Andrew J

State of the Union Addresses of Andrew Johnson

in large print

Andrew Johnson

State of the Union Addresses of Andrew Johnson

in large print

Reproduction of the original.

1st Edition 2023 | ISBN: 978-3-36833-770-4

Verlag (Publisher): Outlook Verlag GmbH, Zeilweg 44, 60439 Frankfurt, Deutschland
Vertretungsberechtigt (Authorized to represent): E. Roepke, Zeilweg 44, 60439 Frankfurt, Deutschland
Druck (Print): Books on Demand GmbH, In de Tarpen 42, 22848 Norderstedt, Deutschland

STATE OF THE UNION ADDRESSES OF ANDREW JOHNSON

By
Andrew Johnson

State of the Union Address
Andrew Johnson
December 4, 1865

Fellow-Citizens of the Senate and House of Representatives:

To express gratitude to God in the name of the people for the preservation of the United States is my first duty in addressing you. Our thoughts next revert to the death of the late President by an act of parricidal treason. The grief of the nation is still fresh. It finds some solace in the consideration that he lived to enjoy the highest proof of its confidence by entering on the renewed term of the Chief Magistracy to which he had been elected; that he brought the civil war substantially to a close; that his loss was deplored in all parts of the Union, and that foreign nations have rendered justice to his memory. His removal cast upon me a heavier weight of cares than ever devolved upon any one of his predecessors. To fulfill my trust I need the support and confidence of all who are associated with me in the various departments of Government and the support and confidence of the people. There is but one way in which I can hope to gain their necessary aid. It is to state with frankness the principles which guide my conduct, and their application to the present state of affairs, well aware that the efficiency of my labors will in a great measure depend on your and their undivided approbation.

The Union of the United States of America was intended by its authors to last as long as the States themselves shall last. "The Union shall be perpetual" are the words of the Confederation. "To form a more perfect Union," by an ordinance of the people of the United States, is the declared purpose of the Constitution. The hand of Divine Providence was never more plainly visible in the affairs of men than in the framing and the adopting of that instrument. It is beyond comparison the greatest event in American history, and, indeed, is it not of all events in modern times the most pregnant with consequences for every people of the earth? The members of the Convention which prepared it brought to their work the experience of the Confederation, of their several States, and of other republican governments, old and new; but they needed and they obtained a wisdom superior to experience. And when for its validity it required the approval of a people that occupied a large part of a continent and acted separately in many distinct conventions, what is more wonderful than that, after earnest contention and long discussion, all feelings and all opinions were ultimately drawn in one way to its support? The Constitution to which life was thus imparted contains within itself ample resources for its own preservation. It has power to enforce the laws, punish treason, and insure domestic tranquillity. In case of the usurpation of the government of a State by one man or an oligarchy, it becomes a duty of the United States to make good the guaranty to that State of a republican form of government, and so to maintain the homogeneousness of all. Does the lapse of time reveal defects? A simple mode of amendment is provided in the Constitution itself, so that its conditions can always be made to conform to the requirements of advancing civilization. No room is allowed even for the thought of a possibility of its coming to an end. And these powers of self-preservation have always been asserted in their complete integrity by every patriotic Chief Magistrate by Jefferson and Jackson not less than by Washington and Madison. The parting advice of the Father of his Country, while yet President, to the people of the United States was that the free Constitution, which was the work of their hands, might be sacredly maintained; and the inaugural words of President Jefferson held up "the preservation of the General Government in its whole constitutional vigor as the sheet anchor of our peace at home and safety abroad." The Constitution is the work of "the people of the United States," and it should be as indestructible as the people.

It is not strange that the framers of the Constitution, which had no model in the past, should not have fully comprehended the excellence of their own work. Fresh from a struggle against arbitrary power, many patriots suffered from harassing fears of an absorption of the State governments by the General Government, and many from a dread that the States would break away from their orbits. But the very greatness of our country should allay the apprehension of encroachments by the General Government. The subjects that come unquestionably within its jurisdiction are so numerous that it must ever naturally refuse to be embarrassed by questions that lie beyond it. Were it otherwise the Executive would sink beneath the burden, the channels of justice would be choked, legislation would be obstructed by excess, so that there is a greater temptation to exercise some of the functions of the General Government through the States than to trespass on their rightful sphere. The "absolute acquiescence in the decisions of the majority" was at the beginning of the century enforced by Jefferson as "the vital principle of republics;" and the events of the last four years have established, we will hope forever, that there lies no appeal to force.

The maintenance of the Union brings with it "the support of the State governments in all their rights," but it is not one of the rights of any State government to renounce its own place in the Union or to nullify the laws of the Union. The largest liberty is to be maintained in the discussion of the acts of the Federal Government, but there is no appeal from its laws except to the various branches of that Government itself, or to the people, who grant to the members of the legislative and of the executive departments no tenure but a limited one, and in that manner always retain the powers of redress.

"The sovereignty of the States" is the language of the Confederacy, and not the language of the Constitution. The latter contains the emphatic words--This Constitution and the laws of the United States which shall be made in pursuance thereof, and all treaties made or which shall be made under the authority of the United States, shall be the supreme law of the land, and the judges in every State shall be bound thereby, anything in the constitution or laws of any State to the contrary notwithstanding. Certainly the Government of the United States is a limited government, and so is every State government a limited government. With us this idea of limitation spreads through every form of administration--general, State, and municipal--and rests on the great distinguishing principle of the recognition of the rights of man. The ancient republics absorbed the individual in the state--prescribed his religion and controlled his activity. The American system rests on the assertion of the equal right of every man to life, liberty, and the pursuit of happiness, to freedom of conscience, to the culture and exercise of all his faculties. As a consequence the State government is limited--as to the General Government in the interest of union, as to the individual citizen in the interest of freedom.

States, with proper limitations of power, are essential to the existence of the Constitution of the United States. At the very commencement, when we assumed a place among the powers of the earth, the Declaration of Independence was adopted by States; so also were the Articles of Confederation: and when "the people of the United States" ordained and established the Constitution it was the assent of the States, one by one, which gave it vitality. In the event, too, of any amendment to the Constitution, the proposition of Congress needs the confirmation of States. Without States one great branch of the legislative government would be wanting. And if we look beyond the letter of the Constitution to the character of our country, its capacity for comprehending within its jurisdiction a vast continental empire is due to the system of States. The best security for the perpetual existence of the States is the "supreme authority" of the Constitution of the United States. The perpetuity of the Constitution brings with it the perpetuity of the States; their mutual relation makes us what we are, and in our political system their connection is indissoluble. The whole can not exist without the parts, nor the parts without the whole. So long as the Constitution of the United States endures, the States will endure. The destruction of the one is the destruction of the other; the preservation of the one is the preservation of the other.

I have thus explained my views of the mutual relations of the Constitution and the States, because they unfold the principles on which I have sought to solve the momentous questions and overcome the appalling difficulties that met me at the very commencement of my Administration. It has been my steadfast object to escape from the sway of momentary passions and to derive a healing policy from the fundamental and unchanging principles of the Constitution.

I found the States suffering from the effects of a civil war. Resistance to the General Government appeared to have exhausted itself. The United States had recovered possession of their forts and arsenals, and their armies were in the occupation of every State which had attempted to secede. Whether the territory within the limits of those States should be held as conquered territory, under military authority emanating from the President as the head of the Army, was the first question that presented itself for decision.

Now military governments, established for an indefinite period, would have offered no security for the early suppression of discontent, would have divided the people into the vanquishers and the vanquished, and would have envenomed hatred rather than have restored affection. Once established, no precise limit to their continuance was conceivable. They would have occasioned an incalculable and exhausting expense. Peaceful emigration to and from that portion of the country is one of the best means that can be thought of for the restoration of harmony, and that emigration would have been prevented; for what emigrant from abroad, what industrious citizen at home, would place himself willingly under military rule? The chief persons who would have followed in the train of the Army would have been dependents on the General Government or men who expected profit from the miseries of their erring fellow-citizens. The powers of patronage and rule which would have been exercised under the President, over a vast and populous and naturally wealthy region are greater than, unless under extreme necessity, I should be willing to intrust to any one man. They are such as, for myself, I could never, unless on occasions of great emergency, consent to exercise. The willful use of such powers, if continued through a period of years, would have endangered the purity of the general administration and the liberties of the States which remained loyal.

Besides, the policy of military rule over a conquered territory would have implied that the States whose inhabitants may have taken part in the rebellion had by the act of those inhabitants ceased to exist. But the true theory is that all pretended acts of secession were from the beginning null and void. The States can not commit treason nor screen the individual citizens who may have committed treason any more than they can make valid treaties or engage in lawful commerce with any foreign power. The States attempting to secede placed themselves in a condition where their vitality was impaired, but not extinguished; their functions suspended, but not destroyed.

But if any State neglects or refuses to perform its offices there is the more need that the General Government should maintain all its authority and as soon as practicable resume the exercise of all its functions. On this principle I have acted, and have gradually and quietly, and by almost imperceptible steps, sought to restore the rightful energy of the General Government and of the States. To that end provisional governors have been appointed for the States, conventions called, governors elected, legislatures assembled, and Senators and Representatives chosen to the Congress of the United States. At the same time the courts of the United States, as far as could be done, have been reopened, so that the laws of the United States may be enforced through their agency. The blockade has been removed and the custom-houses reestablished in ports of entry, so that the revenue of the United States may be collected. The Post-Office Department renews its ceaseless activity, and the General Government is thereby enabled to communicate promptly with its officers and agents. The courts bring security to persons and property; the opening of the ports invites the restoration of industry and commerce; the post-office renews the facilities of social intercourse and of business.

And is it not happy for us all that the restoration of each one of these functions of the General Government brings with it a blessing to the States over which they are extended? Is it not a sure promise of harmony and renewed attachment to the Union that after all that has happened the return of the General Government is known only as a beneficence?

I know very well that this policy is attended with some risk; that for its success it requires at least the acquiescence of the States which it concerns; that it implies an invitation to those States, by renewing their allegiance to the United States, to resume their functions as States of the Union. But it is a risk that must be taken. In the choice of difficulties it is the smallest risk; and to diminish and if possible to remove all danger, I have felt it incumbent on me to assert one other power of the General Government--the power of pardon. As no State can throw a defense over the crime of treason, the power of pardon is exclusively vested in the executive government of the United States. In exercising that power I have taken every precaution to connect it with the clearest recognition of the binding force of the laws of the United States and an unqualified acknowledgment of the great social change of condition in regard to slavery which has grown out of the war.

The next step which I have taken to restore the constitutional relations of the States has been an invitation to them to participate in the high office of amending the

Constitution. Every patriot must wish for a general amnesty at the earliest epoch consistent with public safety. For this great end there is need of a concurrence of all opinions and the spirit of mutual conciliation. All parties in the late terrible conflict must work together in harmony. It is not too much to ask, in the name of the whole people, that on the one side the plan of restoration shall proceed in conformity with a willingness to cast the disorders of the past into oblivion, and that on the other the evidence of sincerity in the future maintenance of the Union shall be put beyond any doubt by the ratification of the proposed amendment to the Constitution, which provides for the abolition of slavery forever within the limits of our country. So long as the adoption of this amendment is delayed, so long will doubt and jealousy and uncertainty prevail. This is the measure which will efface the sad memory of the past; this is the measure which will most certainly call population and capital and security to those parts of the Union that need them most. Indeed, it is not too much to ask of the States which are now resuming their places in the family of the Union to give this pledge of perpetual loyalty and peace. Until it is done the past, however much we may desire it, will not be forgotten, The adoption of the amendment reunites us beyond all power of disruption; it heals the wound that is still imperfectly closed: it removes slavery, the element which has so long perplexed and divided the country; it makes of us once more a united people, renewed and strengthened, bound more than ever to mutual affection and support.

The amendment to the Constitution being adopted, it would remain for the States whose powers have been so long in abeyance to resume their places in the two branches of the National Legislature, and thereby complete the work of restoration. Here it is for you, fellow-citizens of the Senate, and for you, fellow-citizens of the House of Representatives, to judge, each of you for yourselves, of the elections, returns, and qualifications of your own members.

The full assertion of the powers of the General Government requires the holding of circuit courts of the United States within the districts where their authority has been interrupted. In the present posture of our public affairs strong objections have been urged to holding those courts in any of the States where the rebellion has existed; and it was ascertained by inquiry, that the circuit court of the United States would not be held within the district of Virginia during the autumn or early winter, nor until Congress should have "an opportunity to consider and act on the whole subject." To your deliberations the restoration of this branch of the civil authority of the United States is therefore necessarily referred, with the hope that early provision will be made for the resumption of all its functions. It is manifest that treason, most flagrant in character, has been committed. Persons who are charged with its commission should have fair and impartial trials in the highest civil tribunals of the country, in order that the Constitution and the laws may be fully vindicated, the truth dearly established and affirmed that treason is a crime, that traitors should be punished and the offense made infamous, and, at the same time, that the question may be judicially settled, finally and forever, that no State of its own will has the right to renounce its place in the Union.

The relations of the General Government toward the 4,000,000 inhabitants whom the war has called into freedom have engaged my most serious consideration. On the propriety of attempting to make the freedmen electors by the proclamation of the Executive I took for my counsel the Constitution itself, the interpretations of that instrument by its authors and their contemporaries, and recent legislation by Congress. When, at the first movement toward independence, the Congress of the United States instructed the several States to institute governments of their own, they left each State to decide for itself the conditions for the enjoyment of the elective franchise. During the period of the Confederacy there continued to exist a very great diversity in the qualifications of electors in the several States, and even within a State a distinction of qualifications prevailed with regard to the officers who were to be chosen. The Constitution of the United States recognizes these diversities when it enjoins that in the choice of members of the House of

Representatives of the United States "the electors in each State shall have the qualifications requisite for electors of the most numerous branch of the State legislature." After the formation of the Constitution it remained, as before, the uniform usage for each State to enlarge the body of its electors according to its own judgment, and under this system one State after another has proceeded to increase the number of its electors, until now universal suffrage, or something very near it, is the general rule. So fixed was this reservation of power in the habits of the people and so unquestioned has been the interpretation of the Constitution that during the civil war the late President never harbored the purpose--certainly never avowed the purpose--of disregarding it; and in the acts of Congress during that period nothing can be found which, during the continuance of hostilities much less after their close, would have sanctioned any departure by the Executive from a policy which has so uniformly obtained. Moreover, a concession of the elective franchise to the freedmen by act of the President of the United States must have been extended to all colored men, wherever found, and so must have established a change of suffrage in the Northern, Middle, and Western States, not less than in the Southern and Southwestern. Such an act would have created a new class of voters, and would have been an assumption of power by the President which nothing in the Constitution or laws of the United States would have warranted.

On the other hand, every danger of conflict is avoided when the settlement of the question is referred to the several States. They can, each for itself, decide on the measure, and whether it is to be adopted at once and absolutely or introduced gradually and with conditions. In my judgment the freedmen, if they show patience and manly virtues, will sooner obtain a participation in the elective franchise through the States than through the General Government, even if it had power to intervene. When the tumult of emotions that have been raised by the suddenness of the social change shall have subsided, it may prove that they will receive the kindest usage from some of those on whom they have heretofore most closely depended.

But while I have no doubt that now, after the close of the war, it is not competent for the General Government to extend the elective franchise in the several States, it is equally clear that good faith requires the security of the freedmen in their liberty and their property, their right to labor, and their right to claim the just return of their labor. I can not too strongly urge a dispassionate treatment of this subject, which should be carefully kept aloof from all party strife. We must equally avoid hasty assumptions of any natural impossibility for the two races to live side by side in a state of mutual benefit and good will. The experiment involves us in no inconsistency; let us, then, go on and make that experiment in good faith, and not be too easily disheartened. The country is in need of labor, and the freedmen are in need of employment, culture, and protection. While their right of voluntary migration and expatriation is not to be questioned, I would not advise their forced removal and colonization. Let us rather encourage them to honorable and useful industry, where it may be beneficial to themselves and to the country; and, instead of hasty anticipations of the certainty of failure, let there be nothing wanting to the fair trial of the experiment. The change in their condition is the substitution of labor by contract for the status of slavery. The freedman can not fairly be accused of unwillingness to work so long as a doubt remains about his freedom of choice in his pursuits and the certainty of his recovering his stipulated wages. In this the interests of the employer and the employed coincide. The employer desires in his workmen spirit and alacrity, and these can be permanently secured in no other way. And if the one ought to be able to enforce the contract, so ought the other. The public interest will be best promoted if the several States will provide adequate protection and remedies for the freedmen. Until this is in some way accomplished there is no chance for the advantageous use of their labor, and the blame of ill success will not rest on them.

I know that sincere philanthropy is earnest for the immediate realization of its remotest aims; but time is always an element in reform. It is one of the greatest acts on record to have brought 4,000,000 people into freedom. The career of free industry must be fairly opened to them, and then their future prosperity and condition must, after all, rest mainly on themselves. If they fail, and so perish away, let us be careful that the failure shall not be attributable to any denial of justice. In all that relates to the destiny of the freedmen we need not be too anxious to read the future; many incidents which, from a speculative point of view, might raise alarm will quietly settle themselves. Now that slavery is at an end, or near its end, the greatness of its evil in the point of view of public economy becomes more and more apparent. Slavery was essentially a monopoly of labor, and as such locked the States where it prevailed against the incoming of free industry. Where labor was the property of the capitalist, the white man was excluded from employment, or had but the second best chance of finding it; and the foreign emigrant turned away from the region where his condition would be so precarious. With the destruction of the monopoly free labor will hasten from all pans of the civilized world to assist in developing various and immeasurable resources which have hitherto lain dormant. The eight or nine States nearest the Gulf of Mexico have a soil of exuberant fertility, a climate friendly to long life, and can sustain a denser population than is found as yet in any part of our country. And the future influx of population to them will be mainly from the North or from the most cultivated nations in Europe. From the sufferings that have attended them during our late struggle let us look away to the future, which is sure to be laden for them with greater prosperity than has ever before been known. The removal of the monopoly of slave labor is a pledge that those regions will be peopled by a numerous and enterprising population, which will vie with any in the Union in compactness, inventive genius, wealth, and industry.

Our Government springs from and was made for the people--not the people for the Government. To them it owes allegiance; from them it must derive its courage, strength, and wisdom. But while the Government is thus bound to defer to the people, from whom it derives its existence, it should, from the very consideration of its origin, be strong in its power of resistance to the establishment of inequalities. Monopolies, perpetuities, and class legislation are contrary to the genius of free government, and ought not to be allowed. Here there is no room for favored classes or monopolies; the principle of our Government is that of equal laws and freedom of industry. Wherever monopoly attains a foothold, it is sure to be a source of danger, discord, and trouble. We shall but fulfill our duties as legislators by according "equal and exact justice to all men," special privileges to none. The Government is subordinate to the people; but, as the agent and representative of the people, it must be held superior to monopolies, which in themselves ought never to be granted, and which, where they exist, must be subordinate and yield to the Government.

The Constitution confers on Congress the right to regulate commerce among the several States. It is of the first necessity, for the maintenance of the Union, that that commerce should be free and unobstructed. No State can be justified in any device to tax the transit of travel and commerce between States. The position of many States is such that if they were allowed to take advantage of it for purposes of local revenue the commerce between States might be injuriously burdened, or even virtually prohibited. It is best, while the country is still young and while the tendency to dangerous monopolies of this kind is still feeble, to use the power of Congress so as to prevent any selfish impediment to the free circulation of men and merchandise. A tax on travel and merchandise in their transit constitutes one of the worst forms of monopoly, and the evil is increased if coupled with a denial of the choice of route. When the vast extent of our country is considered, it is plain that every obstacle to the free circulation of commerce between the States ought to be sternly guarded against by appropriate legislation within the limits of the Constitution.

The report of the Secretary of the Interior explains the condition of the public lands, the transactions of the Patent Office and the Pension Bureau, the management of our Indian affairs, the progress made in the construction of the

Pacific Railroad, and furnishes information in reference to matters of local interest in the District of Columbia. It also presents evidence of the successful operation of the homestead act, under the provisions of which 1,160,533 acres of the public lands were entered during the last fiscal year--more than one-fourth of the whole number of acres sold or otherwise disposed of during that period. It is estimated that the receipts derived from this source are sufficient to cover the expenses incident to the survey and disposal of the lands entered under this act, and that payments in cash to the extent of from 40 to 50 per cent will be made by settlers who may thus at any time acquire title before the expiration of the period at which it would otherwise vest. The homestead policy was established only after long and earnest resistance; experience proves its wisdom. The lands in the hands of industrious settlers, whose labor creates wealth and contributes to the public resources, are worth more to the United States than if they had been reserved as a solitude for future purchasers.

The lamentable events of the last four years and the sacrifices made by the gallant men of our Army and Navy have swelled the records of the Pension Bureau to an unprecedented extent. On the 30th day of June last the total number of pensioners was 85,986, requiring for their annual pay, exclusive of expenses, the sum of $8,023,445. The number of applications that have been allowed since that date will require a large increase of this amount for the next fiscal year. The means for the payment of the stipends due under existing laws to our disabled soldiers and sailors and to the families of such as have perished in the service of the country will no doubt be cheerfully and promptly granted. A grateful people will not hesitate to sanction any measures having for their object the relief of soldiers mutilated and families made fatherless in the efforts to preserve our national existence.

The report of the Postmaster-General presents an encouraging exhibit of the operations of the Post-Office Department during the year. The revenues of the past year, from the loyal States alone, exceeded the maximum annual receipts from all the States previous to the rebellion in the sum of $6,038,091; and the annual average increase of revenue during the last four years, compared with the revenues of the four years immediately preceding the rebellion, was $3,533,845. The revenues of the last fiscal year amounted to $14,556,158 and the expenditures to $13,694,728, leaving a surplus of receipts over expenditures of $861,430. Progress has been made in restoring the postal service in the Southern States. The views presented by the Postmaster-General against the policy of granting subsidies to the ocean mail steamship lines upon established routes and in favor of continuing the present system, which limits the compensation for ocean service to the postage earnings, are recommended to the careful consideration of Congress.

It appears from the report of the Secretary of the Navy that while at the commencement of the present year there were in commission 530 vessels of all classes and descriptions, armed with 3,000 guns and manned by 51,000 men, the number of vessels at present in commission is 117, with 830 guns and 12,128 men. By this prompt reduction of the naval forces the expenses of the Government have been largely diminished, and a number of vessels purchased for naval purposes from the merchant marine have been returned to the peaceful pursuits of commerce. Since the suppression of active hostilities our foreign squadrons have been reestablished, and consist of vessels much more efficient than those employed on similar service previous to the rebellion. The suggestion for the enlargement of the navy-yards, and especially for the establishment of one in fresh water for ironclad vessels, is deserving of consideration, as is also the recommendation for a different location and more ample grounds for the Naval Academy.

In the report of the Secretary of War a general summary is given of the military campaigns of 1864 and 1865, ending in the suppression of armed resistance to the national authority in the insurgent States. The operations of the general administrative bureaus of the War Department during the past year are detailed and an estimate made of the appropriations that will be required for military purposes in the fiscal year commencing the 1st day of July, 1866. The national military force on the 1st of May, 1865, numbered 1,000,516 men. It is proposed to reduce the military establishment to a peace footing, comprehending 50,000 troops of all arms, organized so as to admit of an enlargement by filling up the ranks to 82,600 if the circumstances of the country should require an augmentation of the Army. The volunteer force has already been reduced by the discharge from service of over 800,000 troops, and the Department is proceeding rapidly in the work of further reduction. The war estimates are reduced from $516,240,131 to $33,814,461, which amount, in the opinion of the Department, is adequate for a peace establishment. The measures of retrenchment in each bureau and branch of the service exhibit a diligent economy worthy of commendation. Reference is also made in the report to the necessity of providing for a uniform militia system and to the propriety of making suitable provision for wounded and disabled officers and soldiers.

The revenue system of the country is a subject of vital interest to its honor and prosperity, and should command the earnest consideration of Congress. The Secretary of the Treasury will lay before you a full and detailed report of the receipts and disbursements of the last fiscal year, of the first quarter of the present fiscal year, of the probable receipts and expenditures for the other three quarters, and the estimates for the year following the 30th of June, 1866. I might content myself with a reference to that report, in which you will find all the information required for your deliberations and decision, but the paramount importance of the subject so presses itself on my own mind that I can not but lay before you my views of the measures which are required for the good character, and I might almost say for the existence, of this people. The life of a republic lies certainly in the energy, virtue, and intelligence of its citizens; but it is equally true that a good revenue system is the life of an organized government. I meet you at a time when the nation has voluntarily burdened itself with a debt unprecedented in our annals. Vast as is its amount, it fades away into nothing when compared with the countless blessings that will be conferred upon our country and upon man by the preservation of the nation's life. Now, on the first occasion of the meeting of Congress since the return of peace, it is of the utmost importance to inaugurate a just policy, which shall at once be put in motion, and which shall commend itself to those who come after us for its continuance. We must aim at nothing less than the complete effacement of the financial evils that necessarily followed a state of civil war. We must endeavor to apply the earliest remedy to the deranged state of the currency, and not shrink from devising a policy which, with-out being oppressive to the people, shall immediately begin to effect a reduction of the debt, and, if persisted in, discharge it fully within a definitely fixed number of years.

It is our first duty to prepare in earnest for our recovery from the ever-increasing evils of an irredeemable currency without a sudden revulsion, and yet without untimely procrastination. For that end we must each, in our respective positions, prepare the way. I hold it the duty of the Executive to insist upon frugality in the expenditures, and a sparing economy is itself a great national resource. Of the banks to which authority has been given to issue notes secured by bonds of the United States we may require the greatest moderation and prudence, and the law must be rigidly enforced when its limits are exceeded. We may each one of us counsel our active and enterprising countrymen to be constantly on their guard, to liquidate debts contracted in a paper currency, and by conducting business as nearly as possible on a system of cash payments or short credits to hold themselves prepared to return to the standard of gold and silver. To aid our fellow-citizens in the prudent management of their monetary affairs, the duty devolves on us to diminish by law the amount of paper money now in circulation. Five years ago the bank-note circulation of the country amounted to not much more than two hundred millions; now the circulation, bank and national, exceeds seven hundred millions. The simple statement of the fact recommends more strongly than any words of mine could do the necessity of our restraining this expansion. The gradual reduction of the currency is the only measure that can save the business of the country from disastrous calamities, and this can be almost imperceptibly accomplished by gradually funding the national circulation in securities that may be made redeemable at the pleasure of the Government.

Our debt is doubly secure--first in the actual wealth and still greater undeveloped resources of the country, and next in the character of our institutions. The most intelligent observers among political economists have not failed to remark that the public debt of a country is safe in proportion as its people are free; that the debt of a republic is the safest of all. Our history confirms and establishes the theory, and is, I firmly believe, destined to give it a still more signal illustration. The secret of this superiority springs not merely from the fact that in a republic the national obligations are distributed more widely through countless numbers in all classes of society; it has its root in the character of our laws. Here all men contribute to the public welfare and bear their fair share of the public burdens. During the war, under the impulses of patriotism, the men of the great body of the people, without regard to their own comparative want of wealth, thronged to our armies and filled our fleets of war, and held themselves ready to offer their lives for the public good. Now, in their turn, the property and income of the country should bear their just proportion of the burden of taxation, while in our impost system, through means of which increased vitality is incidentally imparted to all the industrial interests of the nation, the duties should be so adjusted as to fall most heavily on articles of luxury leaving the necessaries of life as free from taxation as the absolute wants of the Government economically administered will justify. No favored class should demand freedom from assessment, and the taxes should be so distributed as not to fall unduly on the poor, but rather on the accumulated wealth of the country. We should look at the national debt just as it is--not as a national blessing, but as a heavy burden on the industry of the country, to be discharged without unnecessary delay.

It is estimated by the Secretary of the Treasury that the expenditures for the fiscal year ending the 30th of June, 1866, will exceed the receipts $112,194,947. It is gratifying, however, to state that it is also estimated that the revenue for the year ending the 30th of June, 1867, will exceed the expenditures in the sum of $111,682,818. This amount, or so much as may be deemed sufficient for the purpose, may be applied to the reduction of the public debt, which on the 31st day of October, 1865, was $2,740,854,750. Every reduction will diminish the total amount of interest to be paid, and so enlarge the means of still further reductions, until the whole shall be liquidated; and this, as will be seen from the estimates of the Secretary of the Treasury, may be accomplished by annual payments even within a period not exceeding thirty years. I have faith that we shall do all this within a reasonable time; that as we have amazed the world by the suppression of a civil war which was thought to be beyond the control of any government, so we shall equally show the superiority of our institutions by the prompt and faithful discharge of our national obligations.

The Department of Agriculture under its present direction is accomplishing much in developing and utilizing the vast agricultural capabilities of the country, and for information respecting the details of its management reference is made to the annual report of the Commissioner.

I have dwelt thus fully on our domestic affairs because of their transcendent importance. Under any circumstances our great extent of territory and variety of climate, producing almost everything that is necessary for the wants and even the comforts of man, make us singularly independent of the varying policy of foreign powers and protect us against every temptation to "entangling alliances," while at the present moment the reestablishment of harmony and the strength that comes from harmony will be our best security against "nations who feel power and forget right." For myself, it has been and it will be my constant aim to promote peace and amity with all foreign nations and powers, and I have every reason to believe that they all, without exception, are animated by the same disposition.

Our relations with the Emperor of China, so recent in their origin, are most friendly. Our commerce with his dominions is receiving new developments, and it is very pleasing to find that the Government of that great Empire manifests satisfaction with our policy and reposes just confidence in the fairness which marks our intercourse. The unbroken harmony between the United States and the Emperor of Russia is receiving a new support from an enterprise designed to carry telegraphic lines across the continent of Asia, through his dominions, and so to connect us with all Europe by a new channel of intercourse. Our commerce with South America is about to receive encouragement by a direct line of mail steamships to the rising Empire of Brazil. The distinguished party of men of science who have recently left our country to make a scientific exploration of the natural history and rivers and mountain ranges of that region have received from the Emperor that generous welcome which was to have been expected from his constant friendship for the United States and his well-known zeal in promoting the advancement of knowledge. A hope is entertained that our commerce with the rich and populous countries that border the Mediterranean Sea may be largely increased. Nothing will be wanting on the part of this Government to extend the protection of our flag over the enterprise of our fellow-citizens. We receive from the powers in that region assurances of good will; and it is worthy of note that a special envoy has brought us messages of condolence on the

31

death of our late Chief Magistrate from the Bey of Tunis, whose rule includes the old dominions of Carthage, on the African coast.

Our domestic contest, now happily ended, has left some traces in our relations with one at least of the great maritime powers. The formal accordance of belligerent rights to the insurgent States was unprecedented, and has not been justified by the issue. But in the systems of neutrality pursued by the powers which made that concession there was a marked difference. The materials of war for the insurgent States were furnished, in a great measure, from the workshops of Great Britain, and British ships, manned by British subjects and prepared for receiving British armaments, sallied from the ports of Great Britain to make war on American commerce under the shelter of a commission from the insurgent States. These ships, having once escaped from British ports, ever afterwards entered them in every part of the world to refit, and so to renew their depredations. The consequences of this conduct were most disastrous to the States then in rebellion, increasing their desolation and misery by the prolongation of our civil contest. It had, moreover, the effect, to a great extent, to drive the American flag from the sea, and to transfer much of our shipping and our commerce to the very power whose subjects had created the necessity for such a change. These events took place before I was called to the administration of the Government. The sincere desire for peace by which I am animated led me to approve the proposal, already made, to submit the question which had thus arisen between the countries to arbitration. These questions are of such moment that they must have commanded the attention of the great powers, and are so interwoven with the peace and interests of every one of them as to have insured an impartial decision. I regret to inform you that Great Britain declined the arbitrament, but, on the other hand, invited us to the formation of a joint commission to settle mutual claims between the two countries, from which those for the depredations before mentioned should be excluded. The proposition, in that very unsatisfactory form, has been declined.

The United States did not present the subject as an impeachment of the good faith of a power which was professing the most friendly dispositions, but as involving questions of public law of which the settlement is essential to the peace of nations; and though pecuniary reparation to their injured citizens would have followed incidentally on a decision against Great Britain, such compensation was not their primary object. They had a higher motive, and it was in the interests of peace and justice to establish important principles of international law. The correspondence will be placed before you. The ground on which the British minister rests his justification is, substantially, that the municipal law of a nation and the domestic interpretations of that law are the measure of its duty as a neutral, and I feel bound to declare my opinion before you and before the world that that justification can not be sustained before the tribunal of nations. At the same time; I do not advise to any present attempt at redress by acts of legislation. For the future, friendship between the two countries must rest on the basis of mutual justice.

From the moment of the establishment of our free Constitution the civilized world has been convulsed by revolutions in the interests of democracy or of monarchy, but through all those revolutions the United States have wisely and firmly refused to become propagandists of republicanism. It is the only government suited to our condition; but we have never sought to impose it on others, and we have consistently followed the advice of Washington to recommend it only by the careful preservation and prudent use of the blessing. During all the intervening period the policy of European powers and of the United States has, on the whole, been harmonious. Twice, indeed, rumors of the invasion of some parts of America in the interest of monarchy have prevailed; twice my predecessors have had occasion to announce the views of this nation in respect to such interference. On both occasions the remonstrance of the United States was respected from a deep conviction on the part of European Governments that the system of noninterference and mutual abstinence from propagandism was the true rule for the two hemispheres. Since those times we have advanced in wealth and power, but we retain the same purpose to leave the nations of Europe to choose their own dynasties and form their own systems of government. This consistent moderation may justly demand a corresponding moderation. We should regard it as a great calamity to ourselves, to the cause of good government, and to the peace of the world should any European power challenge the American people, as it were, to the defense of republicanism against foreign interference. We can not foresee and are unwilling to consider what opportunities might present themselves, what combinations might offer to protect ourselves against designs inimical to our form of government. The United States desire to act in the future as they have ever acted heretofore; they never will be driven from that course but by the aggression of European powers, and we rely on the wisdom and justice of those powers to respect the system of noninterference which has so long been sanctioned by time, and which by its good results has approved itself to both continents.

The correspondence between the United States and France in reference to questions which have become subjects of discussion between the two Governments will at a proper time be laid before Congress.

When, on the organization of our Government under the Constitution, the President of the United States delivered his inaugural address to the two Houses of Congress, he said to them, and through them to the country and to mankind, that--The preservation of the sacred fire of liberty and the destiny of the republican model of government are justly considered, perhaps, as deeply, as finally, staked on the experiment intrusted to the hands of the American people. And the House of Representatives answered Washington by the voice of Madison: We adore the Invisible Hand which has led the American people, through so many difficulties, to cherish a conscious responsibility for the destiny of republican liberty. More than seventy-six years have glided away since these words were spoken; the United States have passed through severer trials than were foreseen; and now, at this new epoch in our existence as one nation, with our Union purified by sorrows and strengthened by conflict and established by the virtue of the people, the greatness of the occasion invites us once more to repeat with solemnity the pledges of our fathers to hold ourselves answerable before our fellow-men for the success of the republican form of government. Experience has proved its sufficiency in peace and in war; it has vindicated its authority through dangers and afflictions, and sudden and terrible emergencies, which would have crushed any system that had been less firmly fixed in the hearts of the people. At the inauguration of Washington the foreign relations of the country were few and its trade was repressed by hostile regulations; now all the civilized nations of the globe welcome our commerce, and their governments profess toward us amity. Then our country felt its way hesitatingly along an untried path, with States so little bound together by rapid means of communication as to be hardly known to one another, and with historic traditions extending over very few years; now intercourse between the States is swift and intimate; the experience of centuries has been crowded into a few generations, and has created an intense, indestructible nationality. Then our jurisdiction did not reach beyond the inconvenient boundaries of the territory which had achieved independence; now, through cessions of lands, first colonized by Spain and France, the country has acquired a more complex character, and has for its natural limits the chain of lakes, the Gulf of Mexico, and on the east and the west the two great oceans. Other nations were wasted by civil wars for ages before they could establish for themselves the necessary degree of unity; the latent conviction that our form of government is the best ever known to the world has enabled us to emerge from civil war within four years with a complete vindication of the constitutional authority of the General Government and with our local liberties and State institutions unimpaired.

The throngs of emigrants that crowd to our shores are witnesses of the confidence of all peoples in our permanence. Here is the great land of free labor, where industry is blessed with unexampled rewards and the bread of the workingman is sweetened by the consciousness that the cause of the country "is his own cause, his own safety, his own dignity." Here everyone enjoys the free use of his faculties and the choice of activity as a natural right. Here, under the combined influence of a fruitful soil, genial climes, and happy institutions, population has increased fifteen-fold within a century. Here, through the easy development of boundless resources, wealth has increased with twofold greater rapidity than numbers, so that we have become secure against the financial vicissitudes of other countries and, alike in business and in opinion, are self-centered and truly independent. Here more and more care is given to provide education for everyone born on our soil. Here religion, released from political connection with the civil government, refuses to subserve the craft of statesmen, and becomes in its independence the spiritual life of the people. Here toleration is extended to every opinion, in the quiet certainty that truth needs only a fair field to secure the victory. Here the human mind goes forth unshackled in the pursuit of science, to collect stores of knowledge and acquire an ever-increasing mastery over the forces of nature. Here the national domain is offered and held in millions of separate freeholds, so that our fellow-citizens, beyond the occupants of any other part of the earth, constitute in reality a people. Here exists the democratic form of government; and that form of government, by the confession of European statesmen, "gives a power of which no other form is capable, because it incorporates every man with the state and arouses everything that belongs to the soul."

Where in past history does a parallel exist to the public happiness which is within the reach of the people of the United States? Where in any part of the globe can institutions be found so suited to their habits or so entitled to their love as their own free Constitution? Every one of them, then, in whatever part of the land he has his home, must wish its perpetuity. Who of them will not now acknowledge, in the words of Washington, that "every step by which the people of the United States have advanced to the character of an independent nation seems to have been distinguished by some token of providential agency"? Who will not join with me in the prayer that the Invisible Hand which has led us through the clouds that gloomed around our path will so guide us onward to a perfect restoration of fraternal affection that we of this day may be able to transmit our great inheritance of State governments in all their rights, of the General Government in its whole constitutional vigor, to our posterity, and they to theirs through countless generations?

***

State of the Union Address
Andrew Johnson
December 3, 1866

Fellow-Citizens of the Senate and House of Representatives:

After a brief interval the Congress of the United States resumes its annual legislative labors. An all-wise and merciful Providence has abated the pestilence which visited our shores, leaving its calamitous traces upon some portions of our country. Peace, order, tranquillity, and civil authority have been formally declared to exist throughout the whole of the United States. In all of the States civil authority has superseded the coercion of arms, and the people, by their voluntary action, are maintaining their governments in full activity and complete operation. The enforcement of the laws is no longer "obstructed in any State by combinations too powerful to be suppressed by the ordinary course of judicial proceedings," and the animosities engendered by the war are rapidly yielding to the beneficent influences of our free institutions and to the kindly effects of unrestricted social and commercial intercourse. An entire restoration of fraternal feeling must be the earnest wish of every patriotic heart; and we will have accomplished our grandest national achievement when, forgetting the sad events of the past and remembering only their instructive lessons, we resume our onward career as a free, prosperous, and united people.

In my message of the 4th of December, 1865, Congress was informed of the measures which had been instituted by the Executive with a view to the gradual restoration of the States in which the insurrection occurred to their relations with the General Government. Provisional governors had been appointed, conventions called, governors elected, legislatures assembled, and Senators and Representatives chosen to the Congress of the United States. Courts had been opened for the enforcement of laws long in abeyance. The blockade had been removed, custom-houses reestablished, and the internal-revenue laws put in force, in order that the people might contribute to the national income. Postal operations had been renewed, and efforts were being made to restore them to their former condition of efficiency. The States themselves had been asked to take Dart in the high function of amending the Constitution, and of thus sanctioning the extinction of African slavery as one of the legitimate results of our internecine struggle.

Having progressed thus far, the executive department found that it had accomplished nearly all that was within the scope of its constitutional authority. One thing, however, yet remained to be done before the work of restoration could be completed, and that was the admission to Congress of loyal Senators and Representatives from the States whose people had rebelled against the lawful authority of the General Government. This question devolved upon the respective Houses, which by the Constitution are made the judges of the elections, returns, and qualifications of their own members, and its consideration at once engaged the attention of Congress.

In the meantime the executive department--no other plan having been proposed by Congress--continued its efforts to perfect, as far as was practicable, the restoration of the proper relations between the citizens of the respective States, the States, and the Federal Government, extending from time to time, as the public interests seemed to require, the judicial, revenue, and postal systems of the country. With the advice and consent of the Senate, the necessary officers were appointed and appropriations made by Congress for the payment of their salaries. The proposition to amend the Federal Constitution, so as to prevent the existence of slavery within the United States or any place subject to their jurisdiction, was ratified by the requisite number of States, and on the 18th day of December, 1865, it was officially declared to have become valid as a part of the Constitution of the United States. All of the States in which the insurrection had existed promptly amended their constitutions so as to make them conform to the great change thus effected in the organic law of the land; declared null and void all ordinances and laws of secession; repudiated all pretended debts and obligations created for the revolutionary purposes of the insurrection, and proceeded in good faith to the enactment of measures for the protection and amelioration of the condition of the colored race. Congress, however, yet hesitated to admit any of these States to representation, and it was not until toward the close of the eighth month of the session that an exception was made in favor of Tennessee by the admission of her Senators and Representatives.

I deem it a subject of profound regret that Congress has thus far failed to admit to seats loyal Senators and Representatives from the other States whose inhabitants, with those of Tennessee, had engaged in the rebellion. Ten States--more than one-fourth of the whole number--remain without representation; the seats of fifty members in the House of Representatives and of twenty members in the Senate are yet vacant, not by their own consent, not by a failure of election, but by the refusal of Congress to accept their credentials. Their admission, it is believed, would have accomplished much toward the renewal and strengthening of our relations as one people and removed serious cause for discontent on the part of the inhabitants of those States. It would have accorded with the great principle enunciated in the Declaration of American Independence that no people ought to bear the burden of taxation and yet be denied the right of representation. It would have been in consonance with the express provisions of the Constitution that "each

State shall have at least one Representative" and "that no State, without its consent, shall be deprived of its equal suffrage in the Senate." These provisions were intended to secure to every State and to the people of every State the right of representation in each House of Congress; and so important was it deemed by the framers of the Constitution that the equality of the States in the Senate should be preserved that not even by an amendment of the Constitution can any State, without its consent, be denied a voice in that branch of the National Legislature.

It is true it has been assumed that the existence of the States was terminated by the rebellious acts of their inhabitants, and that, the insurrection having been suppressed, they were thenceforward to be considered merely as conquered territories. The legislative, executive, and judicial departments of the Government have, however, with Heat distinctness and uniform consistency, refused to sanction an assumption so incompatible with the nature of our republican system and with the professed objects of the war. Throughout the recent legislation of Congress the undeniable fact makes itself apparent that these ten political communities are nothing less than States of this Union. At the very commencement of the rebellion each House declared, with a unanimity as remarkable as it was significant, that the war was not "waged upon our part in any spirit of oppression, nor for any purpose of conquest or subjugation, nor purpose of overthrowing or interfering with the rights or established institutions of those States, but to defend and maintain the supremacy of the Constitution and all laws made in pursuance thereof, and to preserve the Union, with all the dignity, equality, and rights of the several States unimpaired; and that as soon as these objects" were "accomplished the war ought to cease." In some instances Senators were permitted to continue their legislative functions, while in other instances Representatives were elected and admitted to seats after their States had formally declared their right to withdraw from the Union and were endeavoring to maintain that right by force of arms. All of the States whose people were in insurrection, as States, were included in the apportionment of the direct tax of $20,000,000 annually laid upon the United States by the act approved 5th August, 1861. Congress, by the act of March 4, 1862, and by the apportionment of representation thereunder also recognized their presence as States in the Union; and they have, for judicial purposes, been divided into districts, as States alone can be divided. The same recognition appears in the recent legislation in reference to Tennessee, which evidently rests upon the fact that the functions of the State were not destroyed by the rebellion, but merely suspended; and that principle is of course applicable to those States which, like Tennessee, attempted to renounce their places in the Union.

The action of the executive department of the Government upon this subject has been equally definite and uniform, and the purpose of the war was specifically stated in the proclamation issued by my predecessor on the 22d day of September, 1862. It was then solemnly proclaimed and declared "that hereafter, as heretofore, the war will be prosecuted for the object of practically restoring the constitutional relation between the United States and each of the States and the people thereof in which States that relation is or may be suspended or disturbed."

The recognition of the States by the judicial department of the Government has also been dear and conclusive in all proceedings affecting them as States had in the Supreme, circuit, and district courts. In the admission of Senators and Representatives from any and all of the States there can be no just ground of apprehension that persons who are disloyal will be clothed with the powers of legislation, for this could not happen when the Constitution and the laws are enforced by a vigilant and faithful Congress. Each House is made the "judge of the elections, returns, and qualifications of its own members," and may, "with the concurrence of two-thirds, expel a member." When a Senator or Representative presents his certificate of election, he may at once be admitted or rejected; or, should there be any question as to his eligibility, his credentials may be referred for investigation to the appropriate committee. If admitted to a seat, it must be upon evidence satisfactory to the House of which he thus becomes a member that he possesses the requisite constitutional and legal qualifications. If refused admission as a member for want of due allegiance to the Government and returned to his constituents, they are admonished that none but persons loyal to the United States will be allowed a voice in the legislative councils of the nation, and the political power and moral influence of Congress are thus effectively exerted in the interests of loyalty to the Government and fidelity to the Union. Upon this question, so vitally affecting the restoration of the Union and the permanency of our present form of government, my convictions, heretofore expressed, have undergone no change, but, on the contrary, their correctness has been confirmed by reflection and time. If the admission of loyal members to seats in the respective Houses of Congress was wise and expedient a year ago, it is no less wise and expedient now. If this anomalous condition is right now--if in the exact condition of these States at the present time it is lawful to exclude them from representation--I do not see that the question will be changed by the efflux of time. Ten years hence, if these States remain as they are, the right of representation will be no stronger, the right of exclusion will be no weaker.

The Constitution of the United States makes it the duty of the President to recommend to the consideration of

47

Congress "such measures as he shall judge necessary and expedient." I know of no measure more imperatively demanded by every consideration of national interest, sound policy, and equal justice than the admission of loyal members from the now unrepresented States. This would consummate the work of restoration and exert a most salutary influence in the reestablishment of peace, harmony, and fraternal feeling. It would tend greatly to renew the confidence of the American people in the vigor and stability of their institutions. It would bind us more closely together as a nation and enable us to show to the world the inherent and recuperative power of a government founded upon the will of the people and established upon the principles of liberty, justice, and intelligence. Our increased strength and enhanced prosperity would irrefragably demonstrate the fallacy of the arguments against free institutions drawn from our recent national disorders by the enemies of republican government. The admission of loyal members from the States now excluded from Congress, by allaying doubt and apprehension, would turn capital now awaiting an opportunity for investment into the channels of trade and industry. It would alleviate the present troubled condition of those States, and by inducing emigration aid in the settlement of fertile regions now uncultivated and lead to an increased production of those staples which have added so greatly to the wealth of the nation and commerce of the world. New fields of enterprise would be opened to our progressive people and soon the devastations of war would be repaired and all traces of our domestic differences effaced from the minds of our countrymen.

In our efforts to preserve "the unity of government which constitutes as one people" by restoring the States to the condition which they held prior to the rebellion, we should be cautious, lest, having rescued our nation from perils of threatened disintegration, we resort to consolidation, and in the end absolute despotism, as a remedy for the recurrence of similar troubles. The war having terminated, and with it all occasion for the exercise of powers of doubtful constitutionality, we should hasten to bring legislation within the boundaries prescribed by the Constitution and to return to the ancient landmarks established by our fathers for the guidance of succeeding generations. The constitution which at any time exists till changed by an explicit and authentic act of the whole people is sacredly obligatory upon all. If in the opinion of the people the distribution or modification of the constitutional powers be in any particular wrong, let it be corrected by an amendment in the way which the Constitution designates; but let there be no change by usurpation, for it is the customary weapon by which free governments are destroyed. Washington spoke these words to his countrymen when, followed by their love and gratitude, he voluntarily retired from the cares of public life. "To keep in all things within the pale of our constitutional powers and cherish the Federal Union as the only rock of safety" were prescribed by Jefferson as rules of action to endear to his "countrymen the true principles of their Constitution and promote a union of sentiment and action, equally auspicious to their happiness and safety." Jackson held that the action of the General Government should always be strictly confined to the sphere of its appropriate duties, and justly and forcibly urged that our Government is not to be maintained nor our Union preserved "by invasions of the rights and powers of the several States. In thus attempting to make our General Government strong we make it weak. Its true strength consists in leaving individuals and States as much as possible to themselves; in making itself felt, not in its power, but in its beneficence; not in its control, but in its protection; not in binding the States more closely to the center, but leaving each to move unobstructed in its proper constitutional orbit." These are the teachings of men whose deeds and services have made them illustrious, and who, long since withdrawn from the scenes of life, have left to their country the rich legacy of their example, their wisdom, and their patriotism. Drawing fresh inspiration from their lessons, let us emulate them in love of country and respect for the Constitution and the laws.

The report of the Secretary of the Treasury affords much information respecting the revenue and commerce of the country. His views upon the currency and with reference to a proper adjustment of our revenue system, internal as well as impost, are commended to the careful consideration of Congress. In my last annual message I expressed my general views upon these subjects. I need now only call attention to the necessity of carrying into every department of the Government a system of rigid accountability, thorough retrenchment, and wise economy. With no exceptional nor unusual expenditures, the oppressive burdens of taxation can be lessened by such a modification of our revenue laws as will be consistent with the public faith and the legitimate and necessary wants of the Government.

The report presents a much more satisfactory condition of our finances than one year ago the most sanguine could have anticipated. During the fiscal year ending the 30th June, 1865 (the last year of the war), the public debt was increased $941,902,537, and on the 31st of October, 1865, it amounted to $2,740,854,750. On the 31st day of October, 1866, it had been reduced to $2,552,310,006, the diminution during a period of fourteen months, commencing September 1, 1865, and ending October 31, 1866, having been $206,379,565. In the last annual report on the state of the finances it was estimated that during the three quarters of the fiscal year ending the 30th of June last the debt would be increased $112,194,947. During that period, however, it was reduced $31,196,387, the receipts of the year having been

$89,905,905 more and the expenditures $200,529,235 less than the estimates. Nothing could more clearly indicate than these statements the extent and availability of the national resources and the rapidity and safety with which under our form of government, great military and naval establishments can be disbanded and expenses reduced from a war to a peace footing.

During the fiscal year ending June 30, 1866, the receipts were $558,032,620 and the expenditures $520,750,940, leaving an available surplus of $37,281,680. It is estimated that the receipts for the fiscal year ending the 30th June, 1867, will be $475,061.386, and that the expenditures will reach the sum of $316,428,078, leaving in the Treasury a surplus of $158,633,308. For the fiscal year ending June 30, 1886, it is estimated that the receipts will amount to $436,000,000 and that the expenditures will be $350,247,641, showing an excess of $85,752,359 in favor of the Government. These estimated receipts may be diminished by a reduction of excise and import duties, but after all necessary reductions shall have been made the revenue of the present and of following years will doubtless be sufficient to cover all legitimate charges upon the Treasury and leave a large annual surplus to be applied to the payment of the principal of the debt. There seems now to be no good reason why taxes may not be reduced as the country advances in population and wealth, and yet the debt be extinguished within the next quarter of a century.

The report of the Secretary of War furnishes valuable and important information in reference to the operations of his Department during the past year. Few volunteers now remain in the service, and they are being discharged as rapidly as they can be replaced by regular troops. The Army has been promptly paid, carefully provided with medical treatment, well sheltered and subsisted, and is to be furnished with breech-loading small arms. The military strength of the nation has been unimpaired by the discharge of volunteers, the disposition of unserviceable or perishable stores, and the retrenchment of expenditure. Sufficient war material to meet any emergency has been retained, and from the disbanded volunteers standing ready to respond to the national call large armies can be rapidly organized, equipped, and concentrated. Fortifications on the coast and frontier have received or are being prepared for more powerful armaments; lake surveys and harbor and river improvements are in course of energetic prosecution. Preparations have been made for the payment of the additional bounties authorized during the recent session of Congress, under such regulations as will protect the Government from fraud and secure to the honorably discharged soldier the well-earned reward of his faithfulness and gallantry. More than 6,000 maimed soldiers have received artificial limbs or other surgical apparatus, and 41 national cemeteries, containing the remains of 104,526 Union soldiers, have already been established. The total estimate of military appropriations is $25,205,669.

It is stated in the report of the Secretary of the Navy that the naval force at this time consists of 278 vessels, armed with 2,351 guns. Of these, 115 vessels, carrying 1,029 guns, are in commission, distributed chiefly among seven squadrons. The number of men in the service is 13,600. Great activity and vigilance have been displayed by all the squadrons, and their movements have been judiciously and efficiently arranged in such manner as would best promote American commerce and protect the rights and interests of our countrymen abroad. The vessels unemployed are undergoing repairs or are laid up until their services may be required. Most of the ironclad fleet is at League Island, in the vicinity of Philadelphia, a place which, until decisive action should be taken by Congress, was selected by the Secretary of the Navy as the most eligible location for that class of vessels. It is important that a suitable public station should be provided for the ironclad fleet. It is intended that these vessels shall be in proper condition for any emergency, and it is desirable that the bill accepting League Island for naval purposes, which passed the House of Representatives at its last session, should receive final action at an early period, in order that there may be a suitable public station for this class of vessels, as well as a navy-yard of area sufficient for the wants of the service on the Delaware River. The naval pension fund amounts to $11,750,000, having been increased $2,750,000 during the year. The expenditures of the Department for the fiscal year ending 30th June last were $43,324,526, and the estimates for the coming year amount to $23,568,436. Attention is invited to the condition of our seamen and the importance of legislative measures for their relief and improvement. The suggestions in behalf of this deserving class of our fellow-citizens are earnestly recommended to the favorable attention of Congress.

The report of the Postmaster-General presents a most satisfactory condition of the postal service and submits recommendations which deserve the consideration of Congress. The revenues of the Department for the year ending June 30, 1866, were $14,386,986 and the expenditures $15,352,079, showing an excess of the latter of $965,093. In anticipation of this deficiency, however, a special appropriation was made by Congress in the act approved July 28, 1866. Including the standing appropriation of $700,000 for free mail matter as a legitimate portion of the revenues, yet remaining unexpended, the actual deficiency for the past year is only $265,093--a sum within $51,141 of the amount estimated in the annual report of 1864. The decrease of revenue compared with the previous year was 1 1/5 per cent, and the increase of expenditures, owing principally to the enlargement of the mail service in the South, was 12 per cent. On the 30th of June last there were in operation 6,930 mail routes, with an aggregate length of 180,921 miles, an aggregate annual transportation of 71,837,914 miles, and an aggregate annual cost, including all expenditures, of $8,410,184. The length of railroad routes is 32,092 miles and the annual transportation 30,609,467 miles. The length of steamboat routes is 14,346 miles and the annual transportation 3,411,962 miles. The mail service is rapidly increasing throughout the whole country, and its steady extension in the Southern States indicates their constantly improving condition. The growing importance of the foreign service also merits attention. The post-office department of Great Britain and our own have agreed upon a preliminary basis for a new postal convention, which it is believed will prove eminently beneficial to the commercial interests of the United States, inasmuch as it contemplates a reduction of the international letter postage to one-half the existing rates: a reduction of postage with all other countries to and from which correspondence is transmitted in the British mail, or in closed mails through the United Kingdom; the establishment of uniform and reasonable charges for the sea and territorial transit of correspondence in closed mails; and an allowance to each post-office department of the right to use all mail communications established under the authority of the other for the dispatch of correspondence, either in open or closed mails, on the same terms as those applicable to the inhabitants of the country providing the means of transmission.

The report of the Secretary of the Interior exhibits the condition of those branches of the public service which are committed to his supervision. During the last fiscal year 4,629,312 acres of public land were disposed of, 1,892,516 acres of which were entered under the homestead act. The policy originally adopted relative to the public lands has undergone essential modifications. Immediate revenue, and not their rapid settlement, was the cardinal feature of our land system. Long experience and earnest discussion have resulted in the conviction that the early development of our agricultural resources and the diffusion of an energetic population over our vast territory are objects of far greater importance to the national growth and prosperity than the proceeds of the sale of the land to the highest bidder in open market. The preemption laws confer upon the pioneer who complies with the terms they impose the privilege of purchasing a limited portion of "unoffered lands" at the minimum price. The homestead enactments relieve the settler from the payment of purchase money, and secure him a permanent home upon the condition of residence for a term of years. This liberal policy invites emigration from the Old and from the more crowded portions of the New World. Its propitious results are undoubted, and will be more signally manifested when time shall have given to it a wider development.

Congress has made liberal grants of public land to corporations in aid of the construction of railroads and other internal improvements. Should this policy hereafter prevail, more stringent provisions will be required to secure a faithful application of the fund. The title to the lands should not pass, by patent or otherwise, but remain in the Government and subject to its control until some portion of the road has been actually built. Portions of them might then from time to time be conveyed to the corporation, but never in a greater ratio to the whole quantity embraced by the grant than the completed parts bear to the entire length of the projected improvement. This restriction would not operate to the prejudice of any undertaking conceived in good faith and executed with reasonable energy, as it is the settled practice to withdraw from market the lands falling within the operation of such grants, and thus to exclude the inception of a subsequent adverse right. A breach of the conditions which Congress may deem proper to impose should work a forfeiture of claim to the lands so withdrawn but unconveyed, and of title to the lands conveyed which remain unsold.

Operations on the several lines of the Pacific Railroad have been prosecuted with unexampled vigor and success. Should no unforeseen causes of delay occur, it is confidently anticipated that this great thoroughfare will be completed before the expiration of the period designated by Congress.

During the last fiscal year the amount paid to pensioners, including the expenses of disbursement, was $13,459,996, and 50,177 names were added to the pension rolls. The entire number of pensioners June 30, 1866, was 126,722. This fact furnishes melancholy and striking proof of the sacrifices made to vindicate the constitutional authority of the Federal Government and to maintain inviolate the integrity of the Union They impose upon us corresponding obligations. It is estimated that $33,000,000 will be required to meet the exigencies of this branch of the service during the next fiscal year.

Treaties have been concluded with the Indians, who, enticed into armed opposition to our Government at the outbreak of the rebellion, have unconditionally submitted to our authority and manifested an earnest desire for a renewal of friendly relations.

During the year ending September 30, 1866, 8,716 patents for useful inventions and designs were issued, and at that date the balance in the Treasury to the credit of the patent fund was $228,297.

As a subject upon which depends an immense amount of the production and commerce of the country, I recommend to Congress such legislation as may be necessary for the preservation of the levees of the Mississippi River. It is a matter of national importance that early steps should be taken, not only to add to the efficiency of these barriers against destructive inundations, but for the removal of all obstructions to the free and safe navigation of that great channel of trade and commerce.

The District of Columbia under existing laws is not entitled to that representation in the national councils which from our earliest history has been uniformly accorded to each Territory established from time to time within our limits. It maintains peculiar relations to Congress, to whom the Constitution has granted the power of exercising exclusive legislation over the seat of Government. Our fellow-citizens residing in the District, whose interests are thus confided to the special guardianship of Congress, exceed in number the population of several of our Territories, and no just reason is perceived why a Delegate of their choice should not be admitted to a seat in the House of Representatives. No mode seems so appropriate and effectual of enabling them to make known their peculiar condition and wants and of securing the local legislation adapted to them. I therefore recommend the passage of a law authorizing the electors of the District of Columbia to choose a Delegate, to be allowed the same rights and privileges as a Delegate representing a Territory. The increasing enterprise and rapid progress of improvement in the District are highly gratifying, and I trust that the efforts of the municipal authorities to promote the prosperity of the national metropolis will receive the efficient and generous cooperation of Congress.

The report of the Commissioner of Agriculture reviews the operations of his Department during the past year, and asks the aid of Congress in its efforts to encourage those States which, scourged by war, are now earnestly engaged in the reorganization of domestic industry.

It is a subject of congratulation that no foreign combinations against our domestic peace and safety or our legitimate influence among the nations have been formed or attempted. While sentiments of reconciliation, loyalty, and patriotism have increased at home, a more just consideration of our national character and rights has been manifested by foreign nations.

The entire success of the Atlantic telegraph between the coast of Ireland and the Province of Newfoundland is an achievement which has been justly celebrated in both hemispheres as the opening of an era in the progress of civilization. There is reason to expect that equal success will attend and even greater results follow the enterprise for connecting the two continents through the Pacific Ocean by the projected line of telegraph between Kamchatka and the Russian possessions in America.

The resolution of Congress protesting against pardons by foreign governments of persons convicted of infamous offenses on condition of emigration to our country has been communicated to the states with which we maintain intercourse, and the practice, so justly the subject of complaint on our part, has not been renewed.

The congratulations of Congress to the Emperor of Russia upon his escape from attempted assassination have been presented to that humane and enlightened ruler and received by him with expressions of grateful appreciation.

The Executive, warned of an attempt by Spanish American adventurers to induce the emigration of freedmen of the United States to a foreign country, protested against the project as one which, if consummated, would reduce them to a bondage even more oppressive than that from which they have just been relieved. Assurance has been received from the Government of the State in which the plan was matured that the proceeding will meet neither its encouragement nor approval. It is a question worthy of your consideration whether our laws upon this subject are adequate to the prevention or punishment of the crime thus meditated.

In the month of April last, as Congress is aware, a friendly arrangement was made between the Emperor of France and the President of the United States for the withdrawal from Mexico of the French expeditionary military forces. This withdrawal was to be effected in three detachments, the first of which, it was understood, would leave Mexico in November, now past, the second in March next, and the third and last in November, 1867. Immediately upon the completion of the evacuation the French Government was to assume the same attitude of nonintervention in regard to Mexico as is held by the Government of the United States. Repeated assurances have been given by the Emperor since that agreement that he would complete the promised evacuation within the period mentioned, or sooner.

It was reasonably expected that the proceedings thus contemplated would produce a crisis of great political interest in the Republic of Mexico. The newly appointed minister of the United States, Mr. Campbell, was therefore sent forward on the 9th day of November last to assume his proper functions as minister plenipotentiary of the United States to that Republic. It was also thought expedient that he should be attended in the vicinity of Mexico by the Lieutenant-General of the Army of the United States, with the view of obtaining such information as might be important to determine the course to be pursued by the United States in reestablishing and maintaining necessary and proper intercourse with the Republic of Mexico. Deeply interested in the cause of liberty and humanity, it seemed an obvious duty on our part to exercise whatever influence we possessed for the restoration and permanent establishment in that country of a domestic and republican form of government.

Such was the condition of our affairs in regard to Mexico when, on the 22d of November last, official information was received from Paris that the Emperor of France had some time before decided not to withdraw a detachment of his forces in the month of November past, according to engagement, but that this decision was made with the purpose of withdrawing the whole of those forces in the ensuing spring. Of this determination, however, the United States had not received any notice or intimation, and so soon as the information was received by the Government care was taken to make known its dissent to the Emperor of France.

I can not forego the hope that France will reconsider the subject and adopt some resolution in regard to the evacuation of Mexico which will conform as nearly as practicable with the existing engagement, and thus meet the just expectations of the United States. The papers relating to the subject will be laid before you. It is believed that with the evacuation of Mexico by the expeditionary forces no subject for serious differences between France and the United States would remain. The expressions of the Emperor and people of France warrant a hope that the traditionary friendship between the two countries might in that case be renewed and permanently restored.

A claim of a citizen of the United States for indemnity for spoliations committed on the high seas by the French authorities in the exercise of a belligerent power against Mexico has been met by the Government of France with a proposition to defer settlement until a mutual convention for the adjustment of all claims of citizens and subjects of both countries arising out of the recent wars on this continent shall be agreed upon by the two countries. The suggestion is not deemed unreasonable, but it belongs to Congress to direct the manner in which claims for indemnity by foreigners as well as by citizens of the United States arising out of the late civil war shall be adjudicated and determined. I have no doubt that the subject of all such claims will engage your attention at a convenient and proper time.

It is a matter of regret that no considerable advance has been made toward an adjustment of the differences between the United States and Great Britain arising out of the depredations upon our national commerce and other trespasses committed during our civil war by British subjects, in violation of international law and treaty obligations. The delay, however, may be believed to have resulted in no small degree from the domestic situation of Great Britain. An entire change of ministry occurred in that country during the last session of Parliament. The attention of the new ministry was called to the subject at an early day, and there is some reason to expect that it will now be considered in a becoming and friendly spirit. The importance of an early disposition of the question can not be exaggerated. Whatever might be the wishes of the two Governments, it is manifest that good will and friendship between the two countries can not be established until a reciprocity in the practice of good faith and neutrality shall be restored between the respective nations.

On the 6th of June last, in violation of our neutrality laws, a military expedition and enterprise against the British North American colonies was projected and attempted to be carried on within the territory and jurisdiction of the United States. In obedience to the obligation imposed upon the Executive by the Constitution to see that the laws are faithfully executed, all citizens were warned by proclamation against taking part in or aiding such unlawful proceedings, and the proper civil, military, and naval officers were directed to take all necessary measures for the enforcement of the laws. The expedition failed, but it has not been without its painful consequences. Some of our citizens who, it was alleged, were engaged in the expedition were captured, and have been brought to trial as for a capital offense in the Province of Canada. Judgment and sentence of death have been pronounced against some, while others have been acquitted. Fully believing in the maxim of government that severity of civil punishment for misguided persons who have engaged in revolutionary attempts which have disastrously failed is unsound and unwise, such representations have been made to the British Government in behalf of the convicted persons as, being sustained by an enlightened and humane judgment, will, it is hoped, induce in their cases an exercise of clemency and a judicious amnesty to all who were engaged in the movement. Counsel has been employed by the Government to defend citizens of the United States on trial for capital offenses in Canada, and a discontinuance of the prosecutions which were instituted in the courts of the United States against those who took part in the expedition has been directed.

I have regarded the expedition as not only political in its nature, but as also in a great measure foreign from the United States in its causes, character, and objects. The attempt was understood to be made in sympathy with an insurgent party in Ireland, and by striking at a British Province on this continent was designed to aid in obtaining redress for political grievances which, it was assumed, the people of Ireland had suffered at the hands of the British Government during a period of several centuries. The persons engaged in it were chiefly natives of that country, some of whom had, while others had not, become citizens of the United States under our general laws of naturalization. Complaints of misgovernment in Ireland continually engage the attention of the British nation, and so great an agitation is now prevailing in Ireland that the British Government have deemed it necessary to suspend the writ of habeas corpus in that country. These circumstances must necessarily modify the opinion which we might otherwise have entertained in regard to an expedition expressly prohibited by our neutrality laws. So long as those laws remain upon our statute books they should be faithfully executed, and if they operate harshly, unjustly, or oppressively Congress alone can apply the remedy by their modification or repeal.

Political and commercial interests of the United States are not unlikely to be affected in some degree by events which are transpiring in the eastern regions of Europe, and the time seems to have come when our Government ought to have a proper diplomatic representation in Greece.

This Government has claimed for all persons not convicted or accused or suspected of crime an absolute political right of self-expatriation and a choice of new national allegiance. Most of the European States have dissented from this principle, and have claimed a right to hold such of their subjects as have emigrated to and been naturalized in the United States and afterwards returned on transient visits to their native countries to the performance of military service in like manner as resident subjects. Complaints arising from the claim in this respect made by foreign states have heretofore been matters of controversy between the United States and some of the European powers, and the irritation consequent upon the failure to settle this question increased during the war in which Prussia, Italy, and Austria were recently engaged. While Great Britain has never acknowledged the right of expatriation, she has not for some years past practically insisted upon the opposite doctrine. France has been equally forbearing, and Prussia has proposed a compromise, which, although evincing increased liberality, has not been accepted by the United States. Peace is now prevailing everywhere in Europe, and the present seems to be a favorable time for an assertion by Congress of the principle so long maintained by the executive department that naturalization by one state fully exempts the native-born subject of any other state from the performance of military service under any foreign government, so long as he does not voluntarily renounce its rights and benefits.

In the performance of a duty imposed upon me by the Constitution I have thus submitted to the representatives of the States and of the people such information of our domestic and foreign affairs as the public interests seem to require. Our Government is now undergoing its most trying ordeal, and my earnest prayer is that the peril may be successfully and finally passed without impairing its original strength and symmetry. The interests of the nation are best to be promoted by the revival of fraternal relations, the complete obliteration of our past differences, and the reinauguration of all the pursuits of peace. Directing our efforts to the early accomplishment of these great ends, let us endeavor to preserve harmony between the coordinate departments of the Government, that each in its proper sphere may cordially cooperate with the other in securing the maintenance of the Constitution, the preservation of the Union, and the perpetuity of our free institutions.

***

State of the Union Address
Andrew Johnson
December 3, 1867

Fellow-Citizens of the Senate and House of Representatives:

The continued disorganization of the Union, to which the President has so often called the attention of Congress, is yet a subject of profound and patriotic concern. We may, however, find some relief from that anxiety in the reflection that the painful political situation, although before untried by ourselves, is not new in the experience of nations. Political science, perhaps as highly perfected in our own time and country as in any other, has not yet disclosed any means by which civil wars can be absolutely prevented. An enlightened nation, however, with a wise and beneficent constitution of free government, may diminish their frequency and mitigate their severity by directing all its proceedings in accordance with its fundamental law.

When a civil war has been brought to a close, it is manifestly the first interest and duty of the state to repair the injuries which the war has inflicted, and to secure the benefit of the lessons it teaches as fully and as speedily as possible. This duty was, upon the termination of the rebellion, promptly accepted not only by the executive department, but by the insurrectionary States themselves, and restoration in the first moment of peace was believed to be as easy and certain as it was indispensable. The expectations, however, then so reasonably and confidently entertained were disappointed by legislation from which I felt constrained by my obligations to the Constitution to withhold my assent.

It is therefore a source of profound regret that in complying with the obligation imposed upon the President by the Constitution to give to Congress from time to time information of the state of the Union I am unable to communicate any definitive adjustment satisfactory to the American people, of the questions which since the close of the rebellion have agitated the public mind. On the contrary, candor compels me to declare that at this time there is no Union as our fathers understood the term, and as they meant it to be understood by us. The Union which they established can exist only where all the States are represented in both Houses of Congress; where one State is as free as another to regulate its internal concerns according to its own will, and where the laws of the central Government, strictly confined to matters of national jurisdiction, apply with equal force to all the people of every section. That such is not the present "state of the Union" is a melancholy fact, and we must all acknowledge that the restoration of the States to their proper legal relations with the Federal Government and with one another, according to the terms of the original compact, would be the greatest temporal blessing which God, in His kindest providence, could bestow upon this nation. It becomes our imperative duty to consider whether or not it is impossible to effect this most desirable consummation. The Union and the Constitution are inseparable. As long as one is obeyed by all parties, the other will be preserved; and if one is destroyed, both must perish together. The destruction of the Constitution will be followed by other and still greater calamities. It was ordained not only to form a more perfect union between the States, but to "establish justice, insure domestic tranquillity, provide for the common defense, promote the general welfare, and secure the blessings of liberty to ourselves and our posterity." Nothing but implicit obedience to its requirements in all parts of the country will accomplish these great ends. Without that obedience we can look forward only to continual outrages upon individual rights, incessant breaches of the public peace, national weakness, financial dishonor, the total loss of our prosperity, the general corruption of morals, and the final extinction of popular freedom. To save our country from evils so appalling as these, we should renew our efforts again and again.

To me the process of restoration seems perfectly plain and simple. It consists merely in a faithful application of the Constitution and laws. The execution of the laws is not now obstructed or opposed by physical force. There is no military or other necessity, real or pretended, which can prevent obedience to the Constitution, either North or South. All the rights and all the obligations of States and individuals can be protected and enforced by means perfectly consistent with the fundamental law. The courts may be everywhere open, and if open their process would be unimpeded. Crimes against the United States can be prevented or punished by the proper judicial authorities in a manner entirely practicable and legal. There is therefore no reason why the Constitution should not be obeyed, unless those who exercise its powers have determined that it shall be disregarded and violated. The mere naked will of this Government, or of some one or more of its branches, is the only obstacle that can exist to a perfect union of all the States.

On this momentous question and some of the measures growing out of it I have had the misfortune to differ from Congress, and have expressed my convictions without reserve, though with becoming deference to the opinion of the legislative department. Those convictions are not only unchanged, but strengthened by subsequent events and further reflection The transcendent importance of the subject will be a sufficient excuse for calling your attention to some of the reasons which have so strongly influenced my own judgment. The hope that we may all finally concur in a mode of settlement consistent at once with our true interests and with our sworn duties to the Constitution is too natural and too just to be easily relinquished.

It is clear to my apprehension that the States lately in rebellion are still members of the National Union. When did they cease to be so? The "ordinances of secession" adopted by a portion (in most of them a very small portion) of their citizens were mere nullities. If we admit now that they were valid and effectual for the purpose intended by their authors, we sweep from under our feet the whole ground upon which we justified the war. Were those States afterwards expelled from the Union by the war? The direct contrary was averred by this Government to be its purpose, and was so understood by all those who gave their blood and treasure to aid in its prosecution. It can not be that a successful war, waged for the preservation of the Union, had the legal effect of dissolving it. The victory of the nation's arms was not the disgrace of her policy; the defeat of secession on the battlefield was not the triumph of its lawless principle. Nor could Congress, with or without the consent of the Executive, do anything which would have the effect, directly or indirectly, of separating the States from each other. To dissolve the Union is to repeal the Constitution which holds it together, and that is a power which does not belong to any department of this Government, or to all of them united.

This is so plain that it has been acknowledged by all branches of the Federal Government. The Executive (my predecessor as well as myself) and the heads of all the Departments have uniformly acted upon the principle that the Union is not only undissolved, but indissoluble. Congress submitted an amendment of the Constitution to be ratified by the Southern States, and accepted their acts of ratification as a necessary and lawful exercise of their highest function. If they were not States, or were States out of the Union, their consent to a change in the fundamental law of the Union would have been nugatory, and Congress in asking it committed a political absurdity. The judiciary has also given the solemn sanction of its authority to the same view of the case. The judges of the Supreme Court have included the Southern States in their circuits, and they are constantly, in banc and elsewhere, exercising jurisdiction which does not belong to them unless those States are States of the Union.

If the Southern States are component parts of the Union, the Constitution is the supreme law for them, as it is for all the other States. They are bound to obey it, and so are we. The right of the Federal Government, which is clear and unquestionable, to enforce the Constitution upon them implies the correlative obligation on our part to observe its limitations and execute its guaranties. Without the Constitution we are nothing; by, through, and under the Constitution we are what it makes us. We may doubt the wisdom of the law, we may not approve of its provisions, but we can not violate it merely because it seems to confine our powers within limits narrower than we could wish. It is not a question of individual or class or sectional interest, much less of party predominance, but of duty--of high and sacred duty--which we are all sworn to perform. If we can not support the Constitution with the cheerful alacrity of those who love and believe in it, we must give to it at least the fidelity of public servants who act under solemn obligations and commands which they dare not disregard.

The constitutional duty is not the only one which requires the States to be restored. There is another consideration which, though of minor importance, is yet of great weight. On the 22d day of July, 1861, Congress declared by an almost unanimous vote of both Houses that the war should be conducted solely for the purpose of preserving the Union and maintaining the supremacy of the Federal Constitution and laws, without impairing the dignity, equality, and rights of the States or of individuals, and that when this was done the war should cease. I do not say that this declaration is personally binding on those who joined in making it, any more than individual members of Congress are personally bound to pay a public debt created under a law for which they voted. But it was a solemn public, official pledge of the national honor, and I can not imagine upon what grounds the repudiation of it is to be justified. If it be said that we are not bound to keep faith with rebels, let it be remembered that this promise was not made to rebels only. Thousands of true men in the South were drawn to our standard by it, and hundreds of thousands in the North gave their lives in the belief that it would be carried out. It was made on the day after the first great battle of the war had been fought and lost. All patriotic and intelligent men then saw the necessity of giving such an assurance, and believed that without it the war would end in disaster to our cause. Having given that assurance in the extremity of our peril, the violation of it now, in the day of our power, would be a rude rending of that good faith which holds the moral world together; our country would cease to have any claim upon the confidence of men; it would make the war not only a failure, but a fraud.

Being sincerely convinced that these views are correct, I would be unfaithful to my duty if I did not recommend the repeal of the acts of Congress which place ten of the Southern States under the domination of military masters. If calm reflection shall satisfy a majority of your honorable bodies that the acts referred to are not only a violation of the national faith, but in direct conflict with the Constitution, I dare not permit myself to doubt that you will immediately strike them from the statute book.

To demonstrate the unconstitutional character of those acts I need do no more than refer to their general provisions. It must be seen at once that they are not authorized. To dictate what alterations shall be made in the constitutions of the several States; to control the elections of State legislators and State officers, members of Congress and electors of President and Vice-President, by arbitrarily declaring who shall vote and who shall be excluded from that privilege; to dissolve State legislatures or prevent them from assembling; to dismiss judges and other civil functionaries of the State and appoint others without regard to State law; to organize and operate all the political machinery of the States; to regulate the whole administration of their domestic and local affairs according to the mere will of strange and irresponsible agents, sent among them for that purpose-- these are powers not granted to the Federal Government or to any one of its branches. Not being granted, we violate our trust by assuming them as palpably as we would by acting in the face of a positive interdict; for the Constitution forbids us to do whatever it does not affirmatively authorize, either by express words or by clear implication. If the authority we desire to use does not come to us through the Constitution, we can exercise it only by usurpation, and usurpation is the most dangerous of political crimes. By that crime the enemies of free government in all ages have worked out their designs against public liberty and private right. It leads directly and immediately to the establishment of absolute rule, for undelegated power is always unlimited and unrestrained.

The acts of Congress in question are not only objectionable for their assumption of ungranted power, but many of their provisions are in conflict with the direct prohibitions of the Constitution. The Constitution commands that a republican form of government shall be guaranteed to all the States; that no person shall be deprived of life, liberty, or property without due process of law, arrested without a judicial warrant, or punished without a fair trial before an impartial jury; that the privilege of habeas corpus shall not be denied in time of peace, and that no bill of attainder shall be passed even against a single individual. Yet the system of measures established by these acts of Congress does totally subvert and destroy the form as well as the substance of republican government in the ten States to which they apply. It binds

79

them hand and foot in absolute slavery, and subjects them to a strange and hostile power, more unlimited and more likely to be abused than any other now known among civilized men. It tramples down all those rights in which the essence of liberty consists, and which a free government is always most careful to protect. It denies the habeas corpus and the trial by jury. Personal freedom, property, and life, if assailed by the passion, the prejudice, or the rapacity of the ruler, have no security whatever. It has the effect of a bill of attainder or bill of pains and penalties, not upon a few individuals, but upon whole masses, including the millions who inhabit the subject States, and even their unborn children. These wrongs, being expressly forbidden, can not be constitutionally inflicted upon any portion of our people, no matter how they may have come within our jurisdiction, and no matter whether they live in States, Territories, or districts.

I have no desire to save from the proper and just consequences of their great crime those who engaged in rebellion against the Government, but as a mode of punishment the measures under consideration are the most unreasonable that could be invented. Many of those people are perfectly innocent; many kept their fidelity to the Union untainted to the last; many were incapable of any legal offense; a large proportion even of the persons able to bear arms were forced into rebellion against their will, and of those who are guilty with their own consent the degrees of guilt are as various as the shades of their character and temper. But these acts of Congress confound them all together in one common doom. Indiscriminate vengeance upon classes, sects, and parties, or upon whole communities, for offenses committed by a portion of them against the governments to which they owed obedience was common in the barbarous ages of the world; but Christianity and civilization have made such progress that recourse to a punishment so cruel and unjust would meet with the condemnation of all unprejudiced and right-minded men. The punitive justice of this age, and especially of this country, does not consist in stripping whole States of their liberties and reducing all their people, without distinction, to the condition of slavery. It deals separately with each individual, confines itself to the forms of law, and vindicates its own purity by an impartial examination of every case before a competent judicial tribunal. If this does not satisfy all our desires with regard to Southern rebels, let us console ourselves by reflecting that a free Constitution, triumphant in war and unbroken in peace, is worth far more to us and our children than the gratification of any present feeling.

I am aware it is assumed that this system of government for the Southern States is not to be perpetual. It is true this military government is to be only provisional, but it is through this temporary evil that a greater evil is to be made perpetual. If the guaranties of the Constitution can be broken provisionally to serve a temporary purpose, and in a part only of the country, we can destroy them everywhere and for all time. Arbitrary measures often change, but they generally change for the worse. It is the curse of despotism that it has no halting place. The intermitted exercise of its power brings no sense of security to its subjects, for they can never know what more they will be called to endure when its red right hand is armed to plague them again. Nor is it possible to conjecture how or where power, unrestrained by law, may seek its next victims. The States that are still free may be enslaved at any moment; for if the Constitution does not protect all, it protects none.

It is manifestly and avowedly the object of these laws to confer upon Negroes the privilege of voting and to disfranchise such a number of white citizens as will give the former a clear majority at all elections in the Southern States. This, to the minds of some persons, is so important that a violation of the Constitution is justified as a means of bringing it about. The morality is always false which excuses a wrong because it proposes to accomplish a desirable end. We are not permitted to do evil that good may come. But in this case the end itself is evil, as well as the means. The subjugation of the States to Negro domination would be worse than the military despotism under which they are now suffering. It was believed beforehand that the people would endure any amount of military oppression for any length of time rather than degrade themselves by subjection to the Negro race. Therefore they have been left without a choice. Negro suffrage was established by act of Congress, and the military officers were commanded to superintend the process of clothing the Negro race with the political privileges torn from white men.

The blacks in the South are entitled to be well and humanely governed, and to have the protection of just laws for all their rights of person and property. If it were practicable at this time to give them a Government exclusively their own, under which they might manage their own affairs in their own way, it would become a grave question whether we ought to do so, or whether common humanity would not require us to save them from themselves. But under the circumstances this is only a speculative point. It is not proposed merely that they shall govern themselves, but that they shall rule the white race, make and administer State laws, elect Presidents and members of Congress, and shape to a greater or less extent the future destiny of the whole country. Would such a trust and power be safe in such hands?

The peculiar qualities which should characterize any people who are fit to decide upon the management of public affairs for a great state have seldom been combined. It is the glory of white men to know that they have had these qualities in sufficient measure to build upon this continent a great political fabric and to preserve its stability for more than ninety years, while in every other part of the world all similar experiments have failed. But if anything can be proved by known facts, if all reasoning upon evidence is not abandoned, it must be acknowledged that in the progress of nations Negroes have shown less capacity for government than any other race of people. No independent government of any form has ever been successful in their hands. On the contrary, wherever they have been left to their own devices they have shown a constant tendency to relapse into barbarism. In the Southern States, however, Congress has undertaken to confer upon them the privilege of the ballot. Just released from slavery, it may be doubted whether as a class they know more than their ancestors how to organize and regulate civil society. Indeed, it is admitted that the blacks of the South are not only regardless of the rights of property, but so utterly ignorant of public affairs that their voting can consist in nothing more than carrying a ballot to the place where they are directed to deposit it. I need not remind you that the exercise of the elective franchise is the highest attribute of an American citizen, and that when guided by virtue, intelligence, patriotism, and a proper appreciation of our free institutions it constitutes the true basis of a democratic form of government, in which the sovereign power is lodged in the body of the people. A trust artificially created, not for its own sake, but solely as a means of promoting the general welfare, its influence for good must necessarily depend upon the elevated character and true allegiance of the elector. It ought, therefore, to be reposed in none except those who are fitted morally and mentally to administer it well; for if conferred upon persons who do not justly estimate its value and who are indifferent as to its results, it will only serve as a means of placing power in the hands of the unprincipled and ambitious, and must eventuate in the complete destruction of that liberty of which it should be the most powerful conservator. I have therefore heretofore urged upon your attention the great danger--to be apprehended from an untimely extension of the elective franchise to any new class in our country, especially when the large majority of that class, in wielding the power thus placed in their hands, can not be expected correctly to comprehend the duties and responsibilities which pertain to suffrage. Yesterday, as it were, 4,000,000 persons were held in a condition of slavery that had existed for generations; to-day they are freemen and are assumed by law to be citizens. It can not be presumed, from their previous condition of servitude, that as a class they are as well informed as to the nature of our Government as the intelligent foreigner who makes our land the home of his choice. In the case of the latter neither a residence of five years and the knowledge of our institutions which it gives nor attachment to the principles of the Constitution are the only conditions upon which he can be admitted to citizenship; he must prove in addition a good moral character, and thus give reasonable ground for the belief that he will be faithful to the obligations which he assumes as a citizen of the Republic. Where a people--the source of all political power--speak by their suffrages through the instrumentality of the ballot box, it must be carefully guarded against the control of those who are corrupt in principle and enemies of free institutions, for it can only become to our political and social system a safe conductor of healthy popular sentiment when kept free from demoralizing influences. Controlled through fraud and usurpation by the designing, anarchy and despotism must inevitably follow. In the hands of the patriotic and worthy our Government will be preserved upon the principles of the Constitution inherited from our fathers. It follows, therefore, that in admitting to the ballot box a new class of voters not qualified for the exercise of the elective franchise we weaken our system of government instead of adding to its strength and durability.

I yield to no one in attachment to that rule of general suffrage which distinguishes our policy as a nation. But there is a limit, wisely observed hitherto, which makes the ballot a privilege and a trust, and which requires of some classes a time suitable for probation and preparation. To give it indiscriminately to a new class, wholly unprepared by previous habits and opportunities to perform the trust which it demands, is to degrade it, and finally to destroy its power, for it may be safely assumed that no political truth is better established than that such indiscriminate and all-embracing extension of popular suffrage must end at last in its destruction. I repeat the expression of my willingness to join in any plan within the scope of our constitutional authority which promises to better the condition of the Negroes in the South, by encouraging them in industry, enlightening their minds, improving their morals, and giving protection to all their just rights as freedmen. But the transfer of our political inheritance to them would, in my opinion, be an abandonment of a duty which we owe alike to the memory of our fathers and the rights of our children.

The plan of putting the Southern States wholly and the General Government partially into the hands of Negroes is proposed at a time peculiarly unpropitious. The foundations of society have been broken up by civil war. Industry must be reorganized, justice reestablished, public credit maintained, and order brought out of confusion. To accomplish these ends would require all the wisdom and virtue of the great men who formed our institutions originally. I confidently believe that their descendants will be equal to the arduous task before them, but it is worse than madness to expect that Negroes will perform it for us. Certainly we ought not to ask their assistance till we despair of our own competency.

The great difference between the two races in physical, mental, and moral characteristics will prevent an amalgamation or fusion of them together in one homogeneous mass. If the inferior obtains the ascendency over the other, it will govern with reference only to its own interests for it will recognize no common interest--and create such a tyranny as this continent has never yet witnessed. Already the Negroes are influenced by promises of confiscation and plunder. They are taught to regard as an enemy every white man who has any respect for the rights of his own race. If this continues it must become worse and worse, until all order will be subverted, all industry cease, and the fertile fields of the South grow up into a wilderness. Of all the dangers which our nation has yet encountered, none are equal to those which must result from the success of the effort now making to Africanize the half of our country.

I would not put considerations of money in competition with justice and right; but the expenses incident to "reconstruction" under the system adopted by Congress aggravate what I regard as the intrinsic wrong of the measure itself. It has cost uncounted millions already, and if persisted in will add largely to the weight of taxation, already too oppressive to be borne without just complaint, and may finally reduce the Treasury of the nation to a condition of bankruptcy. We must not delude ourselves. It will require a strong standing army and probably more than $200,000,000 per annum to maintain the supremacy of Negro governments after they are established. The sum thus thrown away would, if properly used, form a sinking fund large enough to pay the whole national debt in less than fifteen years. It is vain to hope that Negroes will maintain their ascendency themselves. Without military power they are wholly incapable of holding in subjection the white people of the South.

I submit to the judgment of Congress whether the public credit may not be injuriously affected by a system of measures like this. With our debt and the vast private interests which are complicated with it, we can not be too cautious of a policy which might by possibility impair the confidence of the world in our Government. That confidence can only be retained by carefully inculcating the principles of justice and honor on the popular mind and by the most scrupulous fidelity to all our engagements of every sort. Any serious breach of the organic law, persisted in for a considerable time, can not but create fears for the stability of our institutions. Habitual violation of prescribed rules, which we bind ourselves to observe, must demoralize the people. Our only standard of civil duty being set at naught, the sheet anchor of our political morality is lost, the public conscience swings from its moorings and yields to every impulse of passion and interest. If we repudiate the Constitution, we will not be expected to care much for mere pecuniary obligations. The violation of such a pledge as we made on the 22d day of July, 1861, will assuredly diminish the market value of our other promises. Besides, if we acknowledge that the national debt was created, not to hold the States in the Union, as the taxpayers were led to suppose, but to expel them from it and hand them over to be governed by Negroes, the moral duty to pay it may seem much less clear. I say it may seem so, for I do not admit that this or any other argument in favor of repudiation can be entertained as sound; but its influence on some classes of minds may well be apprehended. The financial honor of a great commercial nation, largely indebted and with a republican form of government administered by agents of the popular choice, is a thing of such delicate texture and the destruction of it would be followed by such unspeakable calamity that every true patriot must desire to avoid whatever might expose it to the slightest danger.

The great interests of the country require immediate relief from these enactments. Business in the South is paralyzed by a sense of general insecurity, by the terror of confiscation, and the dread of Negro supremacy. The Southern trade, from which the North would have derived so great a profit under a government of law, still languishes, and can never be revived until it ceases to be fettered by the arbitrary power which makes all its operations unsafe. That rich country--the richest in natural resources the world ever saw--is worse than lost if it be not soon placed under the protection of a free constitution. Instead of being, as it ought to be, a source of wealth and power, it will become an intolerable burden upon the rest of the nation.

Another reason for retracing our steps will doubtless be seen by Congress in the late manifestations of public opinion upon this subject. We live in a country where the popular will always enforces obedience to itself, sooner or later. It is vain to think of opposing it with anything short of legal authority backed by overwhelming force. It can not have escaped your attention that from the day on which Congress fairly and formally presented the proposition to govern the Southern States by military force, with a view to the ultimate establishment of Negro supremacy, every expression of the general sentiment has been more or less adverse to it. The affections of this generation can not be detached from the institutions of their ancestors. Their determination to preserve the inheritance of free government in their own hands and transmit it undivided and unimpaired to their own posterity is too strong to be successfully opposed. Every weaker passion will disappear before that love of liberty and law for which the American people are distinguished above all others in the world.

How far the duty of the President "to preserve, protect, and defend the Constitution" requires him to go in opposing an unconstitutional act of Congress is a very serious and important question, on which I have deliberated much and felt extremely anxious to reach a proper conclusion. Where an act has been passed according to the forms of the Constitution by the supreme legislative authority, and is regularly enrolled among the public statutes of the country, Executive resistance to it, especially in times of high party excitement, would be likely to produce violent collision between the respective adherents of the two branches of the Government. This would be simply civil war, and civil war must be resorted to only as the last remedy for the worst of evils. Whatever might tend to provoke it should be most carefully avoided. A faithful and conscientious magistrate will concede very much to honest error, and something even to perverse malice, before he will endanger the public peace; and he will not adopt forcible measures, or such as might lead to force, as long as those which are peaceable remain open to him or to his constituents. It is true that cases may occur in which the Executive would be compelled to stand on its rights, and maintain them regardless of all consequences. If Congress should pass an act which is not only in palpable conflict with the Constitution, but will certainly, if carried out, produce immediate and irreparable injury to the organic structure of the Government, and if there be neither judicial remedy for the wrongs it inflicts nor power in the people to protect themselves without the official aid of their elected defender--if, for instance, the legislative department should pass an act even through all the forms of law to abolish a coordinate department of the Government--in such a case the President must take the high responsibilities of his office and save the life of the nation at all hazards. The so-called reconstruction acts, though as plainly unconstitutional as any that can be imagined, were not believed to be within the class last mentioned. The people were not wholly disarmed of the power of self-defense. In all the Northern States they still held in their hands the sacred right of the ballot, and it was safe to believe that in due time they would come to the rescue of their own institutions. It gives me pleasure to add that the appeal to our common constituents was not taken in vain, and that my confidence in their wisdom and virtue seems not to have been misplaced.

It is well and publicly known that enormous frauds have been perpetrated on the Treasury and that colossal fortunes have been made at the public expense. This species of corruption has increased, is increasing, and if not diminished will soon bring us into total ruin and disgrace. The public creditors and the taxpayers are alike interested in an honest administration of the finances, and neither class will long endure the large-handed robberies of the recent past. For this discreditable state of things there are several causes. Some of the taxes are so laid as to present an irresistible temptation to evade payment. The great sums which officers may win by connivance at fraud create a pressure which is more than the virtue of many can withstand, and there can be no doubt that the open disregard of constitutional obligations avowed by some of the highest and most influential men in the country has greatly weakened the moral sense of those who serve in subordinate places. The expenses of the United States, including interest on the public debt, are more than six times as much as they were seven years ago. To collect and disburse this vast amount requires careful supervision as well as systematic vigilance. The system, never perfected, was much disorganized by the "tenure-of-office bill," which has almost destroyed official accountability. The President may be thoroughly convinced that an officer is incapable, dishonest, or unfaithful to the Constitution, but under the law which I have named the utmost he can do is to complain to the Senate and ask the privilege of supplying his place with a better man. If the Senate be regarded as personally or politically hostile to the President, it is natural, and not altogether unreasonable, for the officer to expect that it will take his part as far as possible, restore him to his place, and give him a triumph over his Executive superior. The officer has other chances of impunity arising from accidental defects of evidence, the mode of investigating it, and the secrecy of the hearing. It is not wonderful that official malfeasance should become bold in proportion as the delinquents learn to think themselves safe. I am entirely persuaded that under such a rule the

President can not perform the great duty assigned to him of seeing the laws faithfully executed, and that it disables him most especially from enforcing that rigid accountability which is necessary to the due execution of the revenue laws.

The Constitution invests the President with authority to decide whether a removal should be made in any given case; the act of Congress declares in substance that he shall only accuse such as he supposes to be unworthy of their trust. The Constitution makes him sole judge in the premises, but the statute takes away his jurisdiction, transfers it to the Senate, and leaves him nothing but the odious and sometimes impracticable duty of becoming a prosecutor. The prosecution is to be conducted before a tribunal whose members are not, like him, responsible to the whole people, but to separate constituent bodies, and who may hear his accusation with great disfavor. The Senate is absolutely without any known standard of decision applicable to such a case. Its judgment can not be anticipated, for it is not governed by any rule. The law does not define what shall be deemed good cause for removal. It is impossible even to conjecture what may or may not be so considered by the Senate. The nature of the subject forbids clear proof. If the charge be incapacity, what evidence will support it? Fidelity to the Constitution may be understood or misunderstood in a thousand different ways, and by violent party men, in violent party times, unfaithfulness to the Constitution may even come to be considered meritorious. If the officer be accused of dishonesty, how shall it be made out? Will it be inferred from acts unconnected with public duty, from private history, or from general reputation, or must the President await the commission of an actual misdemeanor in office? Shall he in the meantime risk the character and interest of the nation in the hands of men to whom he can not give his confidence? Must he forbear his complaint until the mischief is done and can not be prevented? If his zeal in the public service should impel him to anticipate the overt act, must he move at the peril of being tried himself for the offense of slandering his subordinate? In the present circumstances of the country someone must be held responsible for official delinquency of every kind. It is extremely difficult to say where that responsibility should be thrown if it be not left where it has been placed by the Constitution. But all just men will admit that the President ought to be entirely relieved from such responsibility if he can not meet it by reason of restrictions placed by law upon his action.

The unrestricted power of removal from office is a very great one to be trusted even to a magistrate chosen by the general suffrage of the whole people and accountable directly to them for his acts. It is undoubtedly liable to abuse, and at some periods of our history perhaps has been abused. If it be thought desirable and constitutional that it should be so limited as to make the President merely a common informer against other public agents, he should at least be permitted to act in that capacity before some open tribunal, independent of party politics, ready to investigate the merits of every case, furnished with the means of taking evidence, and bound to decide according to established rules. This would guarantee the safety of the accuser when he acts in good faith, and at the same time secure the rights of the other party. I speak, of course, with all proper respect for the present Senate, but it does not seem to me that any legislative body can be so constituted as to insure its fitness for these functions.

It is not the theory of this Government that public offices are the property of those who hold them. They are given merely as a trust for the public benefit, sometimes for a fixed period, sometimes during good behavior, but generally they are liable to be terminated at the pleasure of the appointing power, which represents the collective majesty and speaks the will of the people. The forced retention in office of a single dishonest person may work great injury to the public interests. The danger to the public service comes not from the power to remove, but from the power to appoint. Therefore it was that the framers of the Constitution left the power of removal unrestricted, while they gave the Senate a fight to reject all appointments which in its opinion were not fit to be made. A little reflection on this subject will probably satisfy all who have the good of the country at heart that our best course is to take the Constitution for our guide, walk in the path marked out by the founders of the Republic, and obey the rules made sacred by the observance of our great predecessors.

The present condition of our finances and circulating medium is one to which your early consideration is invited.

The proportion which the currency of any country should bear to the whole value of the annual produce circulated by its means is a question upon which political economists have not agreed. Nor can it be controlled by legislation, but must be left to the irrevocable laws which everywhere regulate commerce and trade. The circulating medium will ever irresistibly flow to those points where it is in greatest demand. The law of demand and supply is as unerring as that which regulates the tides of the ocean; and, indeed, currency, like the tides, has its ebbs and flows throughout the commercial world.

At the beginning of the rebellion the bank-note circulation of the country amounted to not much more than $200,000,000; now the circulation of national-bank notes and those known as "legal-tenders" is nearly seven hundred millions. While it is urged by some that this amount should be increased, others contend that a decided reduction is absolutely essential to the best interests of the country. In view of these diverse opinions, it may be well to ascertain the real value of our paper issues when compared with a metallic or convertible currency. For this purpose let us inquire how much gold and silver could be purchased by the seven hundred millions of paper money now in circulation. Probably not more than half the amount of the latter, showing that when our paper currency is compared with gold and silver its commercial value is compressed into three hundred and fifty millions. This striking fact makes it the obvious duty of the Government, as early as may be consistent with the principles of sound political economy, to take such measures as will enable the holder of its notes and those of the national banks to convert them without loss into specie or its equivalent. A reduction of our paper circulating medium need not necessarily follow. This, however, would depend upon the law of demand and supply, though it should be borne in mind that by making legal-tender and bank notes convertible into coin or its equivalent their present specie value in the hands of their holders would be enhanced 100 per cent.

Legislation for the accomplishment of a result so desirable is demanded by the highest public considerations. The Constitution contemplates that the circulating medium of the country shall be uniform in quality and value. At the time of the formation of that instrument the country had just emerged from the War of the Revolution, and was suffering from the effects of a redundant and worthless paper currency. The sages of that period were anxious to protect their posterity from the evils that they themselves had experienced. Hence in providing a circulating medium they conferred upon Congress the power to coin money and regulate the value thereof, at the same time prohibiting the States from making anything but gold and silver a tender in payment of debts.

The anomalous condition of our currency is in striking contrast with that which was originally designed. Our circulation now embraces, first, notes of the national banks, which are made receivable for all dues to the Government, excluding imposts, and by all its creditors, excepting in payment of interest upon its bonds and the securities themselves; second, legal-tender notes, issued by the United States, and which the law requires shall be received as well in payment of all debts between citizens as of all Government dues, excepting imposts; and, third, gold and silver coin. By the operation of our present system of finance, however, the metallic currency, when collected, is reserved only for one class of Government creditors, who, holding its bonds, semiannually receive their interest in coin from the National Treasury. They are thus made to occupy an invidious position, which may be used to strengthen the arguments of those who would bring into disrepute the obligations of the nation. In the payment of all its debts the plighted faith of the Government should be inviolably maintained. But while it acts with fidelity toward the bondholder who loaned his money that the integrity of the Union might be preserved, it should at the same time observe good faith with the great masses of the people, who, having rescued the Union from the perils of rebellion, now bear the burdens of taxation, that the Government may be able to fulfill its engagements. There is no reason which will be accepted as satisfactory by the people why those who defend us on the land and protect us on the sea; the pensioner upon the gratitude of the nation, bearing the scars and wounds received while in its service; the public servants in the various Departments of the Government; the farmer who supplies the soldiers of the Army and the sailors of the Navy; the artisan who toils in the nation's workshops, or the mechanics and laborers who build its edifices and construct its forts and vessels of war, should, in payment of their just and hard-earned dues, receive depreciated paper, while another class of their countrymen, no more deserving, are paid in coin of gold and silver. Equal and exact justice requires that all the creditors of the Government should be paid in a currency possessing a uniform value. This can only be accomplished by the restoration of the currency to the standard established by the Constitution; and by this means we would remove a discrimination which may, if it has not already done so, create a prejudice that may become deep rooted and widespread and imperil the national credit.

101

The feasibility of making our currency correspond with the constitutional standard may be seen by reference to a few facts derived from our commercial statistics.

The production of precious metals in the United States from 1849 to 1857, inclusive, amounted to $579,000,000; from 1858 to 1860, inclusive, to $137,500,000, and from 1861 to 1867, inclusive, to $457,500,000--making the grand aggregate of products since 1849 $1,174,000,000. The amount of specie coined from 1849 to 1857 inclusive, was $439,000,000; from 1858 to 1860, inclusive, $125,000,000, and from 1861 to 1867, inclusive, $310,000,000--making the total coinage since 1849 $874,000,000. From 1849 to 1857, inclusive, the net exports of specie amounted to $271,000,000; from 1858 to 1860, inclusive, to $148,000,000, and from 1861 to 1867, inclusive, $322,000,000--making the aggregate of net exports since 1849 $741,000,000. These figures show an excess of product over net exports of $433,000,000. There are in the Treasury $111,000,000 in coin, something more than $40,000,000 in circulation on the Pacific Coast, and a few millions in the national and other banks--in all about $160,000,000. This, however, taking into account the specie in the country prior to 1849 leaves more than $300,000,000 which have not been accounted for by exportation, and therefore may yet remain in the country.

These are important facts and show how completely the inferior currency will supersede the better, forcing it from circulation among the masses and causing it to be exported as a mere article of trade, to add to the money capital of foreign lands. They show the necessity of retiring our paper money, that the return of gold and silver to the avenues of trade may be invited and a demand created which will cause the retention at home of at least so much of the productions of our rich and inexhaustible gold-bearing fields as may be sufficient for purposes of circulation. It is unreasonable to expect a return to a sound currency so long as the Government by continuing to issue irredeemable notes fills the channels of circulation with depreciated paper. Notwithstanding a coinage by our mints, since 1849, of $874,000,000, the people are now strangers to the currency which was designed for their use and benefit, and specimens of the precious metals bearing the national device are seldom seen, except when produced to gratify the interest excited by their novelty. If depreciated paper is to be continued as the permanent currency of the country, and all our coin is to become a mere article of traffic and speculation, to the enhancement in price of all that is indispensable to the comfort of the people, it would be wise economy to abolish our mints thus saving the nation the care and expense incident to such establishments, and let all our precious metals be exported in bullion. The time has come, however, when the Government and national banks should be required to take the most efficient steps and make all necessary arrangements for a resumption of specie payments at the earliest practicable period. Specie payments having been once resumed by the Government and banks, all notes or bills of paper issued by either of a less denomination than $20 should by law be excluded from circulation, so that the people may have the benefit and convenience of a gold and silver currency which in all their business transactions will be uniform in value at home and abroad. Every man of property or industry, every man who desires to preserve what he honestly possesses or to obtain what he can honestly earn, has a direct interest in maintaining a safe circulating medium--such a medium as shall be real and substantial, not liable to vibrate with opinions, not subject to be blown up or blown down by the breath of speculation, but to be made stable and secure. A disordered currency is one of the greatest political evils. It undermines the virtues necessary for the support of the social system and encourages propensities destructive of its happiness; it wars against industry, frugality, and economy, and it fosters the evil spirits of extravagance and speculation. It has been asserted by one of our profound and most gifted statesmen that--Of all the contrivances for cheating the laboring classes of mankind, none has been more effectual than that which deludes them with paper money. This is the most effectual of inventions to fertilize the rich man's fields by the sweat of the poor man's brow.

Ordinary tyranny, oppression, excessive taxation--these bear lightly on the happiness of the mass of the community compared with a fraudulent currency and the robberies committed by depreciated paper. Our own history has recorded for our instruction enough, and more than enough, of the demoralizing tendency, the injustice, and the intolerable oppression on the virtuous and well disposed of a degraded paper currency authorized by law or in any way countenanced by government. It is one of the most successful devices, in times of peace or war, expansions or revulsions, to accomplish the transfer of all the precious metals from the great mass of the people into the hands of the few, where they are hoarded in secret places or deposited in strong boxes under bolts and bars, while the people are left to endure all the inconvenience, sacrifice, and demoralization resulting from the use of a depreciated and worthless paper money.

The condition of our finances and the operations of our revenue system are set forth and fully explained in the able and instructive report of the Secretary of the Treasury. On the 30th of June, 1866, the public debt amounted to $2,783,425,879; on the 30th of June last it was $2,692,199,215, showing a reduction during the fiscal year of $91,226,664. During the fiscal year ending June 30, 1867, the receipts were $490,634,010 and the expenditures $346,729,129, leaving an available surplus of $143,904,880.

It is estimated that the receipts for the fiscal year ending June 30, 1868, will be $417,161,928 and that the expenditures will reach the sum of $393,269,226, leaving in the Treasury a surplus of $23,892,702. For the fiscal year ending June 30, 1869, it is estimated that the receipts will amount to $381,000,000 and that the expenditures will be $372,000,000, showing an excess of $9,000,000 in favor of the Government.

The attention of Congress is earnestly invited to the necessity of a thorough revision of our revenue system. Our internal-revenue laws and impost system should be so adjusted as to bear most heavily on articles of luxury, leaving the necessaries of life as free from taxation as may be consistent with the real wants of the Government, economically administered. Taxation would not then fall unduly on the man of moderate means; and while none would be entirely exempt from assessment, all, in proportion to their pecuniary abilities, would contribute toward the support of the State. A modification of the internal-revenue system, by a large reduction in the number of articles now subject to tax, would be followed by results equally advantageous to the citizen and the Government. It would render the execution of the law less expensive and more certain, remove obstructions to industry, lessen the temptations to evade the law, diminish the violations and frauds perpetrated upon its provisions, make its operations less inquisitorial, and greatly reduce in numbers the army of taxgatherers created by the system, who "take from the mouth of honest labor the bread it has earned." Retrenchment, reform, and economy should be carried into every branch of the public service, that the expenditures of the Government may be reduced and the people relieved from oppressive taxation; a sound currency should be restored, and the public faith in regard to the national debt sacredly observed. The accomplishment of these important results, together with the restoration of the Union of the States upon the principles of the Constitution, would inspire confidence at home and abroad in the stability of our institutions and bring to the nation prosperity, peace, and good will.

The report of the Secretary of War ad interim exhibits the operations of the Army and of the several bureaus of the War Department. The aggregate strength of our military force on the 30th of September last was 56,315. The total estimate for military appropriations is $77,124,707, including a deficiency in last year's appropriation of $13,600,000. The payments at the Treasury on account of the service of the War Department from January 1 to October 29, 1867--a period of ten months--amounted to $109,807,000. The expenses of the military establishment, as well as the numbers of the Army, are now three times as great as they have ever been in time of peace, while the discretionary, power is vested in the Executive to add millions to this expenditure by an increase of the Army to the maximum strength allowed by the law.

The comprehensive report of the Secretary of the Interior furnishes interesting information in reference to the important branches of the public service connected with his Department. The menacing attitude of some of the warlike bands of Indians inhabiting the district of country between the Arkansas and Platte rivers and portions of Dakota Territory required the presence of a large military force in that region. Instigated by real or imaginary grievances, the Indians occasionally committed acts of barbarous violence upon emigrants and our frontier settlements; but a general Indian war has been providentially averted. The commissioners under the act of 20th July, 1867, were invested with full power to adjust existing difficulties, negotiate treaties with the disaffected bands, and select for them reservations remote from the traveled routes between the Mississippi and the Pacific. They entered without delay upon the execution of their trust, but have not yet made any official report of their proceedings. It is of vital importance that our distant Territories should be exempt from Indian outbreaks, and that the construction of the Pacific Railroad, an object of national importance, should not be interrupted by hostile tribes. These objects, as well as the material interests and the moral and intellectual improvement of the

Indians, can be most effectually secured by concentrating them upon portions of country set apart for their exclusive use and located at points remote from our highways and encroaching white settlements.

Since the commencement of the second session of the Thirty-ninth Congress 510 miles of road have been constructed on the main line and branches of the Pacific Railway. The line from Omaha is rapidly approaching the eastern base of the Rocky Mountains, while the terminus of the last section of constructed road in California, accepted by the Government on the 24th day of October last, was but 11 miles distant from the summit of the Sierra Nevada. The remarkable energy evinced by the companies offers the strongest assurance that the completion of the road from Sacramento to Omaha will not be long deferred.

During the last fiscal year 7,041,114 acres of public land were disposed of, and the cash receipts from sales and fees exceeded by one-half million dollars the sum realized from those sources during the preceding year. The amount paid to pensioners, including expenses of disbursements, was $18,619,956, and 36,482 names were added to the rolls. The entire number of pensioners on the 30th of June last was 155,474. Eleven thousand six hundred and fifty-five patents and designs were issued during the year ending September 30, 1867, and at that date the balance in the Treasury to the credit of the patent fund was $286,607.

The report of the Secretary of the Navy states that we have seven squadrons actively and judiciously employed, under efficient and able commanders, in protecting the persons and property of American citizens, maintaining the dignity and power of the Government, and promoting the commerce and business interests of our countrymen in every part of the world. Of the 238 vessels composing the present Navy of the United States, 56, carrying 507 guns, are in squadron service. During the year the number of vessels in commission has been reduced 12, and there are 13 less on squadron duty than there were at the date of the last report. A large number of vessels were commenced and in the course of construction when the war terminated, and although Congress had made the necessary appropriations for their completion, the Department has either suspended work upon them or limited the slow completion of the steam vessels, so as to meet the contracts for machinery made with private establishments. The total expenditures of the Navy Department for the fiscal year ending June 30, 1867, were $31,034,011. No appropriations have been made or required since the close of the war for the construction and repair of vessels, for steam machinery, ordnance, provisions and clothing, fuel, hemp, etc., the balances under these several heads having been more than sufficient for current expenditures. It should also be stated to the credit of the Department that, besides asking no appropriations for the above objects for the last two years, the Secretary of the

Navy, on the 30th of September last, in accordance with the act of May 1, 1820, requested the Secretary of the Treasury to carry to the surplus fund the sum of $65,000.000, being the amount received from the sales of vessels and other war property and the remnants of former appropriations.

The report of the Postmaster-General shows the business of the Post-Office Department and the condition of the postal service in a very favorable light, and the attention of Congress is called to its practical recommendations. The receipts of the Department for the year ending June 30, 1867, including all special appropriations for sea and land service and for free mail matter, were $19,978,693. The expenditures for all purposes were $19,235,483, leaving an unexpended balance in favor of the Department of $743,210, which can be applied toward the expenses of the Department for the current year. The increase of postal revenue, independent of specific appropriations, for the year 1867 over that of 1866 was $850,040. The increase of revenue from the sale of stamps and stamped envelopes was $783,404. The increase of expenditures for 1867 over those of the previous year was owing chiefly to the extension of the land and ocean mail service. During the past year new postal conventions have been ratified and exchanged with the United Kingdom of Great Britain and Ireland, Belgium, the Netherlands, Switzerland, the North German Union, Italy, and the colonial government at Hong Kong, reducing very largely the rates of ocean and land postages to and from and within those countries.

The report of the Acting Commissioner of Agriculture concisely presents the condition, wants, and progress of an interest eminently worthy the fostering care of Congress, and exhibits a large measure of useful results achieved during the year to which it refers.

The reestablishment of peace at home and the resumption of extended trade, travel, and commerce abroad have served to increase the number and variety of questions in the Department for Foreign Affairs. None of these questions, however, have seriously disturbed our relations with other states.

The Republic of Mexico, having been relieved from foreign intervention, is earnestly engaged in efforts to reestablish her constitutional system of government. A good understanding continues to exist between our Government and the Republics of Hayti and San Domingo, and our cordial relations with the Central and South American States remain unchanged. The tender, made in conformity with a resolution of Congress, of the good offices of the Government with a view to an amicable adjustment of peace between Brazil and her allies on one side and Paraguay on the other, and between Chile and her allies on the one side and Spain on the other, though kindly received, has in neither case been fully accepted by the belligerents. The war in the valley of the Parana is still vigorously maintained. On the other hand, actual hostilities between the Pacific States and Spain have been more than a year suspended. I shall, on any proper occasion that may occur, renew the conciliatory recommendations which have been already made. Brazil, with enlightened sagacity and comprehensive statesmanship, has opened the great channels of the Amazon and its tributaries to universal commerce. One thing more seems needful to assure a rapid and cheering progress in South America. I refer to those peaceful habits without which states and nations can not in this age well expect material prosperity or social advancement.

The Exposition of Universal Industry at Paris has passed, and seems to have fully realized the high expectations of the French Government. If due allowance be made for the recent political derangement of industry here, the part which the United States has borne in this exhibition of invention and art may be regarded with very high satisfaction. During the exposition a conference was held of delegates from several nations, the United States being one, in which the inconveniences of commerce and social intercourse resulting from the diverse standards of money value were very fully discussed, and plans were developed for establishing by universal consent a common principle for the coinage of gold. These conferences are expected to be renewed, with the attendance of many foreign states not hitherto represented. A report of these interesting proceedings will be submitted to Congress, which will, no doubt, justly appreciate the great object and be ready to adopt any measure which may tend to facilitate its ultimate accomplishment.

On the 25th of February, 1862, Congress declared by law that Treasury notes, without interest, authorized by that act should be legal tender in payment of all debts, public and private, within the United States. An annual remittance of $30,000, less stipulated expenses, accrues to claimants under the convention made with Spain in 1834. These remittances, since the passage of that act, have been paid in such notes. The claimants insist that the Government ought to require payment in coin. The subject may be deemed worthy of your attention.

No arrangement has yet been reached for the settlement of our claims for British depredations upon the commerce of the United States. I have felt it my duty to decline the proposition of arbitration made by Her Majesty's Government, because it has hitherto been accompanied by reservations and limitations incompatible with the rights, interest, and honor of our country. It is not to be apprehended that Great Britain will persist in her refusal to satisfy these just and reasonable claims, which involve the sacred principle of nonintervention--a principle henceforth not more important to the United States than to all other commercial nations.

The West India islands were settled and colonized by European States simultaneously with the settlement and colonization of the American continent. Most of the colonies planted here became independent nations in the close of the last and the beginning of the present century. Our own country embraces communities which at one period were colonies of Great Britain, France, Spain, Holland, Sweden, and Russia. The people in the West Indies, with the exception of those of the island of Hayti, have neither attained nor aspired to independence, nor have they become prepared for self-defense. Although possessing considerable commercial value, they have been held by the several European States which colonized or at some time conquered them, chiefly for purposes of military and naval strategy in carrying out European policy and designs in regard to this continent. In our Revolutionary War ports and harbors in the West India islands were used by our enemy, to the great injury and embarrassment of the United States. We had the same experience in our second war with Great Britain. The same European policy for a long time excluded us even from trade with the West Indies, while we were at peace with all nations. In our recent civil war the rebels and their piratical and blockade-breaking allies found facilities in the same ports for the work, which they too successfully accomplished, of injuring and devastating the commerce which we are now engaged in rebuilding. We labored especially under this disadvantage, that European steam vessels employed by our enemies found friendly shelter, protection, and supplies in West Indian ports, while our naval operations were necessarily carried on from our own distant shores. There was then a universal feeling of the want of an advanced naval outpost between the Atlantic coast and Europe. The duty of obtaining such an outpost peacefully and lawfully, while neither doing nor menacing injury to other states, earnestly engaged the attention of the executive department before the close of the war, and it has not been lost sight of since that time. A not entirely dissimilar naval want revealed itself during the same period on the Pacific coast. The required foothold there was fortunately secured by our late treaty with the Emperor of Russia, and it now seems imperative that the more obvious necessities of the Atlantic coast should not be less carefully provided for. A good and convenient port and harbor, capable of easy defense, will supply that want. With the possession of such a station by the United States, neither we nor any other American nation need longer apprehend injury or offense from any transatlantic enemy. I agree with our early statesmen that the West Indies naturally gravitate to, and may be expected ultimately to be absorbed by, the continental States, including our own. I agree with them also that it is wise to leave the question of such absorption to this process of natural political gravitation. The islands of St. Thomas and St. John, which constitute a part of the group called the Virgin Islands, seemed to offer us advantages immediately desirable, while their acquisition could be secured in harmony with the principles to which I have alluded. A treaty has therefore been concluded with the King of Denmark for the cession of those islands, and will be submitted to the Senate for consideration.

It will hardly be necessary to call the attention of Congress to the subject of providing for the payment to Russia of the sum stipulated in the treaty for the cession of Alaska. Possession having been formally delivered to our commissioner, the territory remains for the present in care of a military force, awaiting such civil organization as shall be directed by Congress.

The annexation of many small German States to Prussia and the reorganization of that country under a new and liberal constitution have induced me to renew the effort to obtain a just and prompt settlement of the long-vexed question concerning the claims of foreign states for military service from their subjects naturalized in the United States.

In connection with this subject the attention of Congress is respectfully called to a singular and embarrassing conflict of laws. The executive department of this Government has hitherto uniformly held, as it now holds, that naturalization in conformity with the Constitution and laws of the United States absolves the recipient from his native allegiance. The courts of Great Britain hold that allegiance to the British Crown is indefensible, and is not absolved by our laws of naturalization. British judges cite courts and law authorities of the United States in support of that theory against the position held by the executive authority of the United States. This conflict perplexes the public mind concerning the rights of naturalized citizens and impairs the national authority abroad. I called attention to this subject in my last annual message, and now again respectfully appeal to Congress to declare the national will unmistakably upon this important question.

The abuse of our laws by the clandestine prosecution of the African slave trade from American ports or by American citizens has altogether ceased, and under existing circumstances no apprehensions of its renewal in this part of the world are entertained. Under these circumstances it becomes a question whether we shall not propose to Her Majesty's Government a suspension or discontinuance of the stipulations for maintaining a naval force for the suppression of that trade.

***

State of the Union Address
Andrew Johnson
December 9, 1868

Fellow-Citizens of the Senate and House of Representatives:

Upon the reassembling of Congress it again becomes my duty to call your attention to the state of the Union and to its continued disorganized condition under the various laws which have been passed upon the subject of reconstruction.

It may be safely assumed as an axiom in the government of states that the greatest wrongs inflicted upon a people are caused by unjust and arbitrary legislation, or by the unrelenting decrees of despotic rulers, and that the timely revocation of injurious and oppressive measures is the greatest good that can be conferred upon a nation. The legislator or ruler who has the wisdom and magnanimity to retrace his steps when convinced of error will sooner or later be rewarded with the respect and gratitude of an intelligent and patriotic people.

Our own history, although embracing a period less than a century, affords abundant proof that most, if not all, of our domestic troubles are directly traceable to violations of the organic law and excessive legislation. The most striking

119

illustrations of this fact are furnished by the enactments of the past three years upon the question of reconstruction. After a fair trial they have substantially failed and proved pernicious in their results, and there seems to be no good reason why they should longer remain upon the statute book. States to which the Constitution guarantees a republican form of government have been reduced to military dependencies in each of which the people have been made subject to the arbitrary will of the commanding general. Although the Constitution requires that each State shall be represented in Congress, Virginia, Mississippi, and Texas are yet excluded from the two Houses, and, contrary to the express provisions of that instrument were denied participation in the recent election for a President and Vice-President of the United States. The attempt to place the white population under the domination of persons of color in the South has impaired, if not destroyed, the kindly relations that had previously existed between them: and mutual distrust has engendered a feeling of animosity which leading in some instances to collision and bloodshed, has prevented that cooperation between the two races so essential to the success of industrial enterprise in the Southern States. Nor have the inhabitants of those States alone suffered from the disturbed condition of affairs growing out of these Congressional enactments. The entire Union has been agitated by grave apprehensions of troubles which might again involve the peace of the nation; its interests have been injuriously affected by the derangement of business and labor, and the consequent want of prosperity throughout that portion of the country.

The Federal Constitution--the magna charta of American rights, under whose wise and salutary provisions we have successfully conducted all our domestic and foreign affairs, sustained ourselves in peace and in war, and become a great nation among the powers of the earth--must assuredly be now adequate to the settlement of questions growing out of the civil war, waged alone for its vindication. This great fact is made most manifest by the condition of the country when Congress assembled in the month of December, 1865. Civil strife had ceased, the spirit of rebellion had spent its entire force, in the Southern States the people had warmed into national life, and throughout the whole country a healthy reaction in public sentiment had taken place. By the application of the simple yet effective provisions of the Constitution the executive department, with the voluntary aid of the States, had brought the work of restoration as near completion as was within the scope of its authority, and the nation was encouraged by the prospect of an early and satisfactory adjustment of all its difficulties. Congress, however, intervened, and, refusing to perfect the work so nearly consummated, declined to admit members from the unrepresented States, adopted a series of measures which arrested the progress of restoration, frustrated all that had been so successfully accomplished, and, after three years of agitation and strife, has left the country further from the attainment of union and fraternal feeling than at the inception of the Congressional plan of reconstruction. It needs no argument to show that legislation which has produced such baneful consequences should be abrogated, or else made to conform to the genuine principles of republican government.

Under the influence of party passion and sectional prejudice, other acts have been passed not warranted by the Constitution. Congress has already been made familiar with my views respecting the "tenure-of-office bill." Experience has proved that its repeal is demanded by the best interests of the country, and that while it remains in force the President can not enjoin that rigid accountability of public officers so essential to an honest and efficient execution of the laws. Its revocation would enable the executive department to exercise the power of appointment and removal in accordance with the original design of the Federal Constitution.

The act of March 2, 1867, making appropriations for the support of the Army for the year ending June 30, 1868, and for other purposes, contains provisions which interfere with the President's constitutional functions as Commander in Chief of the Army and deny to States of the Union the right to protect themselves by means of their own militia. These provisions should be at once annulled; for while the first might, in times of great emergency, seriously embarrass the Executive in efforts to employ and direct the common strength of the nation for its protection and preservation, the other is contrary to the express declaration of the Constitution that "a well-regulated militia being necessary to the security of a free state, the right of the people to keep and bear arms shall not be infringed."

It is believed that the repeal of all such laws would be accepted by the American people as at least a partial return to the fundamental principles of the Government, and an indication that hereafter the Constitution is to be made the nation's safe and unerring guide. They can be productive of no permanent benefit to the country, and should not be permitted to stand as so many monuments of the deficient wisdom which has characterized our recent legislation.

The condition of our finances demands the early and earnest consideration of Congress. Compared with the growth of our population, the public expenditures have reached an amount unprecedented in our history.

The population of the United States in 1790 was nearly 4,000,000 people. Increasing each decade about 33 per cent, it reached in 1860 31,000,000, an increase of 700 per cent on the population in 1790. In 1869 it is estimated that it will reach 38,000,000, or an increase of 868 per cent in seventy-nine years.

The annual expenditures of the Federal Government in 1791 were $4,200,000; in 1820, $18.200,000; in 1850, forty-one millions; in 1860, sixty-three millions; in 1865, nearly thirteen hundred millions; and in 1869 it is estimated by the Secretary of the Treasury, in his last annual report, that they will be three hundred and seventy-two millions.

By comparing the public disbursements of 1869, as estimated, with those of 1791, it will be seen that the increase of expenditure since the beginning of the Government has been 8,618 per cent, while the increase of the population for the same period was only 868 per cent. Again, the expenses of the Government in 1860, the year of peace immediately preceding the war, were only sixty--three millions, while in 1869, the year of peace three years after the war it is estimated they will be three hundred and seventy-two millions, an increase of 489 per cent, while the increase of population was only 21 per cent for the same period.

These statistics further show that in 1791 the annual national expenses, compared with the population, were little more than $1 per capita, and in 1860 but $2 per capita; while in 1869 they will reach the extravagant sum of $9.78 per capita.

It will be observed that all these statements refer to and exhibit the disbursements of peace periods. It may, therefore, be of interest to compare the expenditures of the three war periods--the war with Great Britain, the Mexican War, and the War of the Rebellion.

In 1814 the annual expenses incident to the War of 1812 reached their highest amount--about thirty-one millions-- while our population slightly exceeded 8,000,000, showing an expenditure of only $3.80 per capita. In 1847 the expenditures growing out of the war with Mexico reached fifty-five millions, and the population about 21,000,000, giving only $2.60 per capita for the war expenses of that year. In 1865 the expenditures called for by the rebellion reached the vast amount of twelve hundred and ninety millions, which, compared with a population of 34,000,000, gives $38.20 per capita.

From the 4th day of March, 1789, to the 30th of June, 1861, the entire expenditures of the Government were $1,700,000,000. During that period we were engaged in wars with Great Britain and Mexico, and were involved in hostilities with powerful Indian tribes; Louisiana was purchased from France at a cost of $15,000,000; Florida was ceded to us by Spain for five millions; California was acquired from Mexico for fifteen millions, and the territory of New Mexico was obtained from Texas for the sum of ten millions. Early in 1861 the War of the Rebellion commenced;

and from the 1st of July of that year to the 30th of June, 1865, the public expenditures reached the enormous aggregate of thirty-three hundred millions. Three years of peace have intervened, and during that time the disbursements of the Government have successively been five hundred and twenty millions, three hundred and forty-six millions, and three hundred and ninety-three millions. Adding to these amounts three hundred and seventy-two millions, estimated as necessary for the fiscal year ending the 30th of June, 1869, we obtain a total expenditure of $1,600,000,000 during the four years immediately succeeding the war, or nearly as much as was expended during the seventy-two years that preceded the rebellion and embraced the extraordinary expenditures already named.

These startling facts clearly illustrate the necessity of retrenchment in all branches of the public service. Abuses which were tolerated during the war for the preservation of the nation will not be endured by the people, now that profound peace prevails. The receipts from internal revenues and customs have during the past three years gradually diminished, and the continuance of useless and extravagant expenditures will involve us in national bankruptcy, or else make inevitable an increase of taxes already too onerous and in many respects obnoxious on account of their inquisitorial character. One hundred millions annually are expended for the military force, a large portion of which is employed in the execution of laws both unnecessary and unconstitutional; one hundred and fifty millions are required each year to pay the interest on the public debt: an army of taxgatherers impoverishes the nation, and public agents, placed by Congress beyond the control of the Executive, divert from their legitimate purposes large sums of money which they collect from the people in the name of the Government. Judicious legislation and prudent economy can alone remedy defects and avert evils which, if suffered to exist, can not fail to diminish confidence in the public councils and weaken the attachment and respect of the people toward their political institutions. Without proper care the small balance which it is estimated will remain in the Treasury at the close of the present fiscal year will not be realized, and additional millions be added to a debt which is now enumerated by billions.

It is shown by the able and comprehensive report of the Secretary of the Treasury that the receipts for the fiscal year ending June 30, 1868, were $405,638,083, and that the expenditures for the same period were $377,340,284, leaving in the Treasury a surplus of $28,297,798. It is estimated that the receipts during the present fiscal year, ending June 30, 1869, will be $341,392,868 and the expenditures $336,152,470, showing a small balance of $5,240,398 in favor of the Government. For the fiscal year ending June 30, 1870, it is estimated that the receipts will amount to $327,000,000 and the expenditures to $303,000,000, leaving an estimated surplus of $24,000,000.

It becomes proper in this connection to make a brief reference to our public indebtedness, which has accumulated with such alarming rapidity and assumed such colossal proportions.

In 1789, when the Government commenced operations under the Federal Constitution, it was burdened with an indebtedness of $75,000,000, created during the War of the Revolution. This amount had been reduced to $45,000,000 when, in 1812, war was declared against Great Britain. The three years' struggle that followed largely increased the national obligations, and in 1816 they had attained the sum of $127,000,000. Wise and economical legislation, however, enabled the Government to pay the entire amount within a period of twenty years, and the extinguishment of the national debt filled the land with rejoicing and was one of the great events of President Jackson's Administration. After its redemption a large fund remained in the Treasury, which was deposited for safe-keeping with the several States. on condition that it should be returned when required by the public wants. In 1849--the year after the termination of an expensive war with Mexico--we found ourselves involved in a debt of $64,000,000; and this was the amount owed by the Government in 1860, just prior to the outbreak of the rebellion. In the spring of 1861 our civil war commenced.

Each year of its continuance made an enormous addition to the debt: and when in the spring of 1865, the nation successfully emerged from the conflict, the obligations of the Government had reached the immense sum of $2.873,992,909. The Secretary of the Treasury shows that on the 1st day of November, 1867, this amount had been reduced to $2,491,504,450; but at the same time his report exhibits an increase during the past year of $35,625,102, for the debt on the 1st day of November last is stated to have been $2,527,129,552. It is estimated by the Secretary that the returns for the past month will add to our liabilities the further sum of $11,000,000, making a total increase during thirteen months of $46,500,000.

In my message to Congress December 4, 1865, it was suggested that a policy should be devised which, without being oppressive to the people, would at once begin to effect a reduction of the debt, and, if persisted in, discharge it fully within a definite number of years. The Secretary of the Treasury forcibly recommends legislation of this character, and justly urges that the longer it is deferred the more difficult must become its accomplishment. We should follow the wise precedents established in 1789 and 1816, and without further delay make provision for the payment of our obligations at as early a period as may be practicable. The fruits of their labors should be enjoyed by our citizens rather than used to build up and sustain moneyed monopolies in our own and other lands. Our foreign debt is already computed by the Secretary of the Treasury at $850,000,000; citizens of foreign countries receive interest upon a large portion of our securities, and American taxpayers are made to contribute large sums for their support. The idea that such a debt is to become permanent should be at all times discarded as involving taxation too heavy to be borne, and payment once in every sixteen years, at the present rate of interest, of an amount equal to the original sum. This vast debt, if permitted to become permanent and increasing, must eventually be gathered into the hands of a few, and enable them to exert a dangerous and controlling power in the affairs of the Government. The borrowers would become servants to the lenders, the lenders the masters of the people. We now pride ourselves upon having given freedom to 4,000,000 of the colored race; it will then be our shame that 40,000,000 of people, by their own toleration of usurpation and profligacy, have suffered themselves to become enslaved, and merely exchanged slave owners for new taskmasters in the shape of bondholders and taxgatherers. Besides, permanent debts pertain to monarchical governments, and, tending to monopolies, perpetuities, and class legislation, are totally irreconcilable with free institutions introduced into our republican system, they would gradually but surely sap its foundations, eventually subvert our governmental fabric, and erect upon its ruins a moneyed aristocracy. It is our sacred duty to transmit unimpaired to our posterity the blessings of liberty which were bequeathed to us by the founders of the Republic. and by our example teach those who are to follow us carefully to avoid the dangers which threaten a free and independent people.

Various plans have been proposed for the payment of the public debt. However they may have varied as to the time and mode in which it should be redeemed, there seems to be a general concurrence as to the propriety and justness of a reduction in the present rate of interest. The Secretary of the Treasury in his report recommends 5 per cent; Congress, in a bill passed prior to adjournment on the 27th of July last, agreed upon 4 and 4 1/2 per cent; while by many 3 per cent has been held to be an amply sufficient return for the investment. The general impression as to the exorbitancy of the existing rate of interest has led to an inquiry in the public mind respecting the consideration which the Government has actually received for its bonds, and the conclusion is becoming prevalent that the amount which it obtained was in real money three or four hundred per cent less than the obligations which it issued in return. It can not be denied that we are paying an extravagant percentage for the use of the money borrowed, which was paper currency, greatly depreciated below the value of coin. This fact is made apparent when we consider that bondholders receive from the Treasury upon each dollar they own in Government securities 6 per cent in gold, which is nearly or quite equal to 9 per cent in currency; that the bonds are then converted into capital for the national banks, upon which those institutions issue their circulation, bearing 6 per cent interest; and that they are exempt from taxation by the Government and the States, and thereby enhanced 2 per cent in the hands of the holders. We thus have an aggregate of 17 per cent which may be received upon each dollar by the owners of Government securities. A system that produces such results is justly regarded as favoring a few at the expense of the many, and has led to the further inquiry whether our bondholders, in view of the large profits which they have enjoyed, would themselves be averse to a settlement of our indebtedness upon a plan which would yield them a fair remuneration and at the same time be just to the taxpayers of the nation. Our national credit should be sacredly observed, but in making provision for our creditors we should not forget what is due to the masses of the people. It may be assumed that the holders of our securities have already received upon their bonds a larger amount than their original investment, measured by a gold standard. Upon this statement of facts it would seem but just and equitable that the 6 per cent interest now paid by the Government should be applied to the reduction of the principal in semiannual installments, which in sixteen years and eight months would liquidate the entire national debt. Six per cent in gold would at present rates be equal to 9 per cent in currency, and equivalent to the payment of the debt one and a half times in a fraction less than seventeen years. This, in connection with all the other advantages derived from their investment, would afford to the public creditors a fair and liberal compensation for the use of their capital, and with this they should be satisfied. The lessons of the past admonish the lender that it is not well to be over-anxious in exacting from the borrower rigid compliance with the letter of the bond.

If provision be made for the payment of the indebtedness of the Government in the manner suggested, our nation will rapidly recover its wonted prosperity. Its interests require that some measure should be taken to release the large amount of capital invested in the securities of the Government. It is not now merely unproductive, but in taxation annually consumes $150,000,000, which would otherwise be used by our enterprising people in adding to the wealth of the nation. Our commerce, which at one time successfully rivaled that of the great maritime powers, has rapidly diminished, and our industrial interests are in a depressed and languishing condition. The development of our inexhaustible resources is checked, and the fertile fields of the South are becoming waste for want of means to till them. With the release of capital, new life would be infused into the paralyzed energies of our people and activity and vigor imparted to every branch of industry. Our people need encouragement in their efforts to recover from the effects of the rebellion and of injudicious legislation, and it should be the aim of the Government to stimulate them by the prospect of an early release from the burdens which impede their prosperity. If we can not take the burdens from their shoulders, we should at least manifest a willingness to help to bear them.

In referring to the condition of the circulating medium, I shall merely reiterate substantially that portion of my last annual message which relates to that subject.

The proportion which the currency of any country should bear to the whole value of the annual produce circulated by its means is a question upon which political economists have not agreed. Nor can it be controlled by legislation, but must be left to the irrevocable laws which everywhere regulate commerce and trade. The circulating medium will ever irresistibly flow to those points where it is in greatest demand. The law of demand and supply is as unerring as that which regulates the tides of the ocean; and, indeed, currency, like the tides, has its ebbs and flows throughout the commercial world.

At the beginning of the rebellion the bank-note circulation of the country amounted to not much more than $200,000,000; now the circulation of national-bank notes and those known as "legal-tenders" is nearly seven hundred millions. While it is urged by some that this amount should be increased, others contend that a decided reduction is absolutely essential to the best interests of the country. In view of these diverse opinions, it may be well to ascertain the real value of our paper issues when compared with a metallic or convertible currency. For this purpose let us inquire how much gold and silver could be purchased by the seven hundred millions of paper money now in circulation. Probably not more than half the amount of the latter; showing that when our paper currency is compared with gold and silver its commercial value is compressed into three hundred and fifty millions. This striking fact makes it the obvious duty of the Government, as early as may be consistent with the principles of sound political economy, to take such measures as will enable the holders of its notes and those of the national banks to convert them, without loss, into specie or its equivalent. A reduction of our paper circulating medium need not necessarily follow. This, however, would depend upon the law of demand and supply, though it should be borne in mind that by making legal-tender and bank notes convertible into coin or its equivalent their present specie value in the hands of their holders would be enhanced 100 per cent.

Legislation for the accomplishment of a result so desirable is demanded by the highest public considerations. The Constitution contemplates that the circulating medium of the country shall be uniform in quality and value. At the time of the formation of that instrument the country had just emerged from the War of the Revolution, and was suffering from the effects of a redundant and worthless paper currency. The sages of that period were anxious to protect their posterity from the evils which they themselves had experienced. Hence in providing a circulating medium they conferred upon Congress the power to coin money and regulate the value thereof, at the same time prohibiting the States from making anything but gold and silver a tender in payment of debts.

The anomalous condition of our currency is in striking contrast with that which was originally designed. Our circulation now embraces, first, notes of the national banks, which are made receivable for all dues to the Government, excluding imposts, and by all its creditors, excepting in payment of interest upon its bonds and the securities themselves; second, legal tender, issued by the United States, and which the law requires shall be received as well in payment of all debts between citizens as of all Government dues, excepting imposts; and, third, gold and silver coin. By the operation of our present system of finance however, the metallic currency, when collected, is reserved only for one class of Government creditors, who, holding its bonds, semiannually receive their interest in coin from the National Treasury. There is no reason which will be accepted as satisfactory by the people why those who defend us on the land and protect us on the sea; the pensioner upon the gratitude of the nation, bearing the scars and wounds received while in its service; the public servants in the various departments of the Government; the farmer who supplies the soldiers of the Army and the sailors of the Navy; the artisan who toils in the nation's workshops, or the mechanics and laborers who build its edifices and construct its forts and vessels of war, should, in payment of their just and hard-earned dues, receive depreciated paper, while another class of their countrymen, no more deserving are paid in coin of gold and silver. Equal and exact justice requires that all the creditors of the Government should be paid in a currency possessing a uniform value. This can only be accomplished by the restoration of the currency to the standard established by the Constitution, and by this means we would remove a discrimination which may, if it has not already done so, create a prejudice that may become deep-rooted and widespread and imperil the national credit.

The feasibility of making our currency correspond with the constitutional standard may be seen by reference to a few facts derived from our commercial statistics.

The aggregate product of precious metals in the United States from 1849 to 1867 amounted to $1,174,000,000, while for the same period the net exports of specie were $741,000,000. This shows an excess of product over net exports of $433,000,000. There are in the Treasury $103,407,985 in coin; in circulation in the States on the Pacific Coast about $40,000,000, and a few millions in the national and other banks--in all less than $160,000,000. Taking into consideration the specie in the country prior to 1849 and that produced since 1867, and we have more than $300,000,000 not accounted for by exportation or by returns of the Treasury, and therefore most probably remaining in the country.

These are important facts, and show how completely the inferior currency will supersede the better, forcing it from circulation among the masses and causing it to be exported as a mere article of trade, to add to the money capital of foreign lands. They show the necessity of retiring our paper money, that the return of gold and silver to the avenues of trade may be invited and a demand created which will cause the retention at home of at least so much of the productions of our rich and inexhaustible gold-bearing fields as may be sufficient for purposes of circulation. It is unreasonable to expect a return to a sound currency so long as the Government and banks, by continuing to issue irredeemable notes, fill the channels of circulation with depreciated paper. Notwithstanding a coinage by our mints since 1849 of $874,000,000, the people are now strangers to the currency which was designed for their use and benefit, and specimens of the precious metals bearing the national device are seldom seen, except when produced to gratify the interest excited by their novelty. If depreciated paper is to be continued as the permanent currency of the country, and all our coin is to become a mere article of traffic and speculation to the enhancement in price of all that is indispensable to the comfort of the people, it would be wise economy to abolish our mints, thus saving the nation the care and expense incident to such establishments, and let our precious metals be exported in bullion. The time has come, however, when the Government and national banks should be required to take the most efficient steps and make all necessary arrangements for a resumption of specie payments. Let specie payments once be earnestly inaugurated by the Government and banks, and the value of the paper circulation would directly approximate a specie standard.

Specie payments having been resumed by the Government and banks, all notes or bills of paper issued by either of a less denomination than $20 should by law be excluded from circulation, so that the people may have the benefit and convenience of a gold and silver currency which in all their business transactions will be uniform in value at home and abroad. Every man of property or industry, every man who desires to preserve what he honestly possesses or to obtain what he can honestly earn, has a direct interest in maintaining a safe circulating medium--such a medium as shall be real and substantial, not liable to vibrate with opinions, not subject to be blown up or blown down by the breath of speculation, but to be made stable and secure. A disordered currency is one of the greatest political evils. It undermines the virtues necessary for the support of the social system and encourages propensities destructive of its happiness; it wars against industry, frugality, and economy, and it fosters the evil spirits of extravagance and speculation. It has been asserted by one of our profound and most gifted statesmen that--Of all the contrivances for cheating the laboring classes of mankind, none has been more effectual than that which deludes them with paper money. This is the most effectual of inventions to fertilize the rich man's fields by the sweat of the poor man's brow. Ordinary tyranny, oppression, excessive taxation--these bear lightly on the happiness of the mass of the community compared with a fraudulent currency and the robberies committed by depreciated paper. Our own history has recorded for our instruction enough, and more than enough, of the demoralizing tendency, the injustice, and the intolerable oppression on the virtuous and well-disposed of a degraded paper currency authorized by law or in any way countenanced by government. It is one of the most successful devices, in times of peace or war, of expansions or revulsions, to accomplish the transfer of all the precious metals from the great mass of the people into the hands of the few, where they are hoarded in secret places or deposited under bolts and bars, while the people are left to endure all the inconvenience, sacrifice, and demoralization resulting from the use of depreciated and worthless paper.

The Secretary of the Interior in his report gives valuable information in reference to the interests confided to the supervision of his Department, and reviews the operations of the Land Office, Pension Office, Patent Office, and Indian Bureau.

During the fiscal year ending June 30. 1868, 6,655,700 acres of public land were disposed of. The entire cash receipts of the General Land Office for the same period were $1,632,745, being greater by $284,883 than the amount realized from the same sources during the previous year. The entries under the homestead law cover 2,328,923 acres, nearly one-fourth of which was taken under the act of June 21, 1866, which applies only to the States of Alabama, Mississippi, Louisiana, Arkansas, and Florida.

On the 30th of June, 1868, 169,643 names were borne on the pension rolls, and during the year ending on that day the total amount paid for pensions, including the expenses of disbursement, was $24,010,982, being $5,391,025 greater than that expended for like purposes during the preceding year.

During the year ending the 30th of September last the expenses of the Patent Office exceeded the receipts by $171, and, including reissues and designs, 14,153 patents were issued.

Treaties with various Indian tribes have been concluded, and will be submitted to the Senate for its constitutional action. I cordially sanction the stipulations which provide for reserving lands for the various tribes, where they may be encouraged to abandon their nomadic habits and engage in agricultural and industrial pursuits. This policy, inaugurated many years since, has met with signal success whenever it has been pursued in good faith and with becoming liberality by the United States. The necessity for extending it as far as practicable in our relations with the aboriginal population is greater now than at any preceding period. Whilst we furnish subsistence and instruction to the Indians and guarantee the undisturbed enjoyment of their treaty rights, we should habitually insist upon the faithful observance of their agreement to remain within their respective reservations. This is the only mode by which collisions with other tribes and with the whites can be avoided and the safety of our frontier settlements secured.

The companies constructing the railway from Omaha to Sacramento have been most energetically engaged in prosecuting the work, and it is believed that the line will be completed before the expiration of the next fiscal year. The 6 per cent bonds issued to these companies amounted on the

5th instant to $44,337,000, and additional work had been performed to the extent of $3,200,000.

The Secretary of the Interior in August last invited my attention to the report of a Government director of the Union Pacific Railroad Company who had been specially instructed to examine the location, construction, and equipment of their road. I submitted for the opinion of the Attorney-General certain questions in regard to the authority of the Executive which arose upon this report and those which had from time to time been presented by the commissioners appointed to inspect each successive section of the work. After carefully considering the law of the case, he affirmed the right of the Executive to order, if necessary, a thorough revision of the entire road. Commissioners were thereupon appointed to examine this and other lines, and have recently submitted a statement of their investigations, of which the report of the Secretary of the Interior furnishes specific information.

The report of the Secretary of War contains information of interest and importance respecting the several bureaus of the War Department and the operations of the Army. The strength of our military force on the 30th of September last was 48,000 men, and it is computed that by the 1st of January next this number will be decreased to 43,000. It is the opinion of the Secretary of War that within the next year a considerable diminution of the infantry force may be made without detriment to the interests of the country; and in view of the great expense attending the military peace establishment and the absolute necessity of retrenchment wherever it can be applied, it is hoped that Congress will sanction the reduction which his report recommends. While in 1860 sixteen thousand three hundred men cost the nation $16,472,000, the sum of $65,682,000 is estimated as necessary for the support of the Army during the fiscal year ending June 30, 1870. The estimates of the War Department for the last two fiscal years were, for 1867, $33,814,461, and for 1868 $25,205,669. The actual expenditures during the same periods were, respectively, $95,224,415 and $123,246,648. The estimate submitted in December last for the fiscal year ending June 30, 1869, was $77,124,707; the expenditures for the first quarter, ending the 30th of September last, were $27,219,117, and the Secretary of the Treasury gives $66,000,000 as the amount which will probably be required during the remaining three quarters, if there should be no reduction of the Army--making its aggregate cost for the year considerably in excess of ninety-three millions. The difference between the estimates and expenditures for the three fiscal years which have been named is thus shown to be $175,545,343 for this single branch of the public service.

The report of the Secretary of the Navy exhibits the operations of that Department and of the Navy during the year. A considerable reduction of the force has been effected. There are 42 vessels, carrying 411 guns, in the six squadrons which are established in different parts of the world. Three of these vessels are returning to the United States and 4 are used as storeships, leaving the actual cruising force 35 vessels, carrying 356 guns. The total number of vessels in the Navy is 206, mounting 1,743 guns. Eighty-one vessels of every description are in use, armed with 696 guns. The number of enlisted men in the service, including apprentices, has been reduced to 8,500. An increase of navy-yard facilities is recommended as a measure which will in the event of war be promotive of economy and security. A more thorough and systematic survey of the North Pacific Ocean is advised in view of our recent acquisitions, our expanding commerce, and the increasing intercourse between the Pacific States and Asia. The naval pension fund, which consists of a moiety of the avails of prizes captured during the war, amounts to $14,000,000. Exception is taken to the act of 23d July last, which reduces the interest on the fund loaned to the Government by the Secretary, as trustee, to 3 per cent instead of 6 per cent, which was originally stipulated when the investment was made. An amendment of the pension laws is suggested to remedy omissions and defects in existing enactments. The expenditures of the Department during the last fiscal year were $20,120,394, and the estimates for the coming year amount to $20,993,414.

The Postmaster-General's report furnishes a full and clear exhibit of the operations and condition of the postal service. The ordinary postal revenue for the fiscal year ending June 30, 1868. was $16,292,600, and the total expenditures, embracing all the service for which special appropriations have been made by Congress, amounted to $22,730,592, showing an excess of expenditures of $6,437,991. Deducting from the expenditures the sum of $1,896,525, the amount of appropriations for ocean-steamship and other special service, the excess of expenditures was $4,541,466. By using an unexpended balance in the Treasury of $3,800,000 the actual sum for which a special appropriation is required to meet the deficiency is $741,466. The causes which produced this large excess of expenditure over revenue were the restoration of service in the late insurgent States and the putting into operation of new service established by acts of Congress, which amounted within the last two years and a half to about 48,700 miles--equal to more than one-third of the whole amount of the service at the close of the war. New postal conventions with Great Britain, North Germany, Belgium, the Netherlands, Switzerland, and Italy, respectively, have been carried into effect. Under their provisions important improvements have resulted in reduced rates of international postage and enlarged mail facilities with European countries. The cost of the United States transatlantic ocean mail service since January 1, 1868, has been largely lessened under the operation of these new conventions, a reduction of over one-half having been effected under the new arrangements for ocean mail steamship service which went into effect on that date. The attention of Congress is invited to the practical suggestions and recommendations made in his report by the Postmaster-General.

No important question has occurred during the last year in our accustomed cordial and friendly intercourse with Costa Rica, Guatemala, Honduras, San Salvador, France, Austria, Belgium, Switzerland, Portugal, the Netherlands, Denmark, Sweden and Norway, Rome, Greece, Turkey, Persia, Egypt, Liberia, Morocco, Tripoli, Tunis, Muscat, Siam, Borneo, and Madagascar.

Cordial relations have also been maintained with the Argentine and the Oriental Republics. The expressed wish of Congress that our national good offices might be tendered to those Republics, and also to Brazil and Paraguay, for bringing to an end the calamitous war which has so long been raging in the valley of the La Plata, has been assiduously complied with and kindly acknowledged by all the belligerents. That important negotiation, however, has thus far been without result.

Charles A. Washburn, late United States minister to Paraguay, having resigned, and being desirous to return to the United States, the rear-admiral commanding the South

Atlantic Squadron was early directed to send a ship of war to Asuncion, the capital of Paraguay, to receive Mr. Washburn and his family and remove them from a situation which was represented to be endangered by faction and foreign war. The Brazilian commander of the allied invading forces refused permission to the Wasp to pass through the blockading forces, and that vessel returned to its accustomed anchorage. Remonstrance having been made against this refusal, it was promptly overruled, and the Wasp therefore resumed her errand, received Mr. Washburn and his family, and conveyed them to a safe and convenient seaport. In the meantime an excited controversy had arisen between the President of Paraguay and the late United States minister, which, it is understood, grew out of his proceedings in giving asylum in the United States legation to alleged enemies of that Republic. The question of the right to give asylum is one always difficult and often productive of great embarrassment. In states well organized and established, foreign powers refuse either to concede or exercise that right, except as to persons actually belonging to the diplomatic service. On the other hand, all such powers insist upon exercising the right of asylum in states where the law of nations is not fully acknowledged, respected, and obeyed.

The President of Paraguay is understood to have opposed to Mr. Washburn's proceedings the injurious and very improbable charge of personal complicity in insurrection and treason. The correspondence, however, has not yet reached the United States.

Mr. Washburn, in connection with this controversy, represents that two United States citizens attached to the legation were arbitrarily seized at his side, when leaving the capital of Paraguay, committed to prison, and there subjected to torture for the purpose of procuring confessions of their own criminality and testimony to support the President's allegation against the United States minister. Mr. McMahon, the newly appointed minister to Paraguay, having reached the La Plata, has been instructed to proceed without delay to Asuncion, there to investigate the whole subject. The rear-admiral commanding the United States South Atlantic Squadron has been directed to attend the new minister with a proper naval force to sustain such just demands as the occasion may require, and to vindicate the rights of the United States citizens referred to and of any others who may be exposed to danger in the theater of war. With these exceptions, friendly relations have been maintained between the United States and Brazil and Paraguay.

Our relations during the past year with Bolivia, Ecuador, Peru, and Chile have become especially friendly and cordial. Spain and the Republics of Peru, Bolivia, and Ecuador have expressed their willingness to accept the mediation of the United States for terminating the war upon the South Pacific coast. Chile has not finally declared upon the question. In the meantime the conflict has practically exhausted itself, since no belligerent or hostile movement has been made by either party during the last two years, and there are no indications of a present purpose to resume hostilities on either side. Great Britain and France have cordially seconded our proposition of mediation, and I do not forego the hope that it may soon be accepted by all the belligerents and lead to a secure establishment of peace and friendly relations between the Spanish American Republics of the Pacific and Spain--a result which would be attended with common benefits to the belligerents and much advantage to all commercial nations. I communicate, for the consideration of Congress, a correspondence which shows that the Bolivian Republic has established the extremely liberal principle of receiving into its citizenship any citizen of the United States, or of any other of the American Republics, upon the simple condition of voluntary registry.

The correspondence herewith submitted will be found painfully replete with accounts of the ruin and wretchedness produced by recent earthquakes, of unparalleled severity, in the Republics of Peru, Ecuador, and Bolivia. The diplomatic agents and naval officers of the United States who were present in those countries at the time of those disasters furnished all the relief in their power to the sufferers, and were promptly rewarded with grateful and touching acknowledgments by the Congress of Peru. An appeal to the charity of our fellow-citizens has been answered by much liberality. In this connection I submit an appeal which has been made by the Swiss Republic, whose Government and institutions are kindred to our own, in behalf of its inhabitants, who are suffering extreme destitution, produced by recent devastating inundations.

Our relations with Mexico during the year have been marked by an increasing growth of mutual confidence. The Mexican Government has not yet acted upon the three treaties celebrated here last summer for establishing the rights of naturalized citizens upon a liberal and just basis, for regulating consular powers, and for the adjustment of mutual claims.

All commercial nations, as well as all friends of republican institutions, have occasion to regret the frequent local disturbances which occur in some of the constituent States of Colombia. Nothing has occurred, however, to affect the harmony and cordial friendship which have for several years existed between that youthful and vigorous Republic and our own.

Negotiations are pending with a view to the survey and construction of a ship canal across the Isthmus of Darien, under the auspices of the United States. I hope to be able to submit the results of that negotiation to the Senate during its present session.

The very liberal treaty which was entered into last year by the United States and Nicaragua has been ratified by the latter Republic.

Costa Rica, with the earnestness of a sincerely friendly neighbor, solicits a reciprocity of trade, which I commend to the consideration of Congress.

The convention created by treaty between the United States and Venezuela in July, 1865, for the mutual adjustment of claims, has been held, and its decisions have been received at the Department of State. The heretofore-recognized Government of the United States of Venezuela has been subverted. A provisional government having been instituted under circumstances which promise durability, it has been formally recognized.

I have been reluctantly obliged to ask explanation and satisfaction for national injuries committed by the President of Hayti. The political and social condition of the Republics of Hayti and St. Domingo is very unsatisfactory and painful. The abolition of slavery, which has been carried into effect throughout the island of St. Domingo and the entire West Indies, except the Spanish islands of Cuba and Porto Rico, has been followed by a profound popular conviction of the rightfulness of republican institutions and an intense desire to secure them. The attempt, however, to establish republics there encounters many obstacles, most of which may be supposed to result from long-indulged habits of colonial supineness and dependence upon European monarchical powers. While the United States have on all occasions professed a decided unwillingness that any part of this continent or of its adjacent islands shall be made a theater for a new establishment of monarchical power, too little has been done by us, on the other hand, to attach the communities by which we are surrounded to our own country, or to lend even a moral support to the efforts they are so resolutely and so constantly making to secure republican institutions for themselves. It is indeed a question of grave consideration whether our recent and present example is not calculated to check the growth and expansion of free principles, and make those communities distrust, if not dread, a government which at will consigns to military domination States that are integral parts of our Federal Union, and, while ready to resist any attempts by other nations to extend to this hemisphere the monarchical institutions of Europe, assumes to establish over a large portion of its people a rule more absolute, harsh, and tyrannical than any known to civilized powers.

The acquisition of Alaska was made with the view of extending national jurisdiction and republican principles in the American hemisphere. Believing that a further step could be taken in the same direction, I last year entered into a treaty with the King of Denmark for the purchase of the islands of St. Thomas and St. John, on the best terms then attainable, and with the express consent of the people of those islands. This treaty still remains under consideration in the Senate. A new convention has been entered into with Denmark, enlarging the time fixed for final ratification of the original treaty.

Comprehensive national policy would seem to sanction the acquisition and incorporation into our Federal Union of the several adjacent continental and insular communities as speedily as it can be done peacefully, lawfully, and without any violation of national justice, faith, or honor. Foreign possession or control of those communities has hitherto hindered the growth and impaired the influence of the United States. Chronic revolution and anarchy there would be equally injurious. Each one of them, when firmly established as an independent republic, or when incorporated into the United States, would be a new source of strength and power. Conforming my Administration to these principles, I have or no occasion lent support or toleration to unlawful expeditions set on foot upon the plea of republican propagandism or of national extension or aggrandizement. The necessity, however, of repressing such unlawful movements clearly indicates the duty which rests upon us of adapting our legislative action to the new circumstances of a decline of European monarchical power and influence and the increase of American republican ideas, interests, and sympathies.

It can not be long before it will become necessary for this Government to lend some effective aid to the solution of the political and social problems which are continually kept before the world by the two Republics of the island of St. Domingo, and which are now disclosing themselves more distinctly than heretofore in the island of Cuba. The subject is commended to your consideration with all the more earnestness because I am satisfied that the time has arrived when even so direct a proceeding as a proposition for an annexation of the two Republics of the island of St. Domingo would not only receive the consent of the people interested, but would also give satisfaction to all other foreign nations.

I am aware that upon the question of further extending our possessions it is apprehended by some that our political system can not successfully be applied to an area more extended than our continent; but the conviction is rapidly gaining ground in the American mind that with the increased facilities for intercommunication between all portions of the earth the principles of free government, as embraced in our Constitution, if faithfully maintained and carried out, would prove of sufficient strength and breadth to comprehend within their sphere and influence the civilized nations of the world.

The attention of the Senate and of Congress is again respectfully invited to the treaty for the establishment of commercial reciprocity with the Hawaiian Kingdom entered into last year, and already ratified by that Government. The attitude of the United States toward these islands is not very different from that in which they stand toward the West Indies. It is known and felt by the Hawaiian Government and people that their Government and institutions are feeble and precarious; that the United States, being so near a neighbor, would be unwilling to see the islands pass under foreign control. Their prosperity is continually disturbed by expectations and alarms of unfriendly political proceedings, as well from the United States as from other foreign powers. A reciprocity treaty, while it could not materially diminish the revenues of the United States, would be a guaranty of the good will and forbearance of all nations until the people of the islands shall of themselves, at no distant day, voluntarily apply for admission into the Union.

The Emperor of Russia has acceded to the treaty negotiated here in January last for the security of trade-marks in the interest of manufacturers and commerce. I have invited his attention to the importance of establishing, now while it seems easy and practicable, a fair and equal regulation of the vast fisheries belonging to the two nations in the waters of the North Pacific Ocean.

The two treaties between the United States and Italy for the regulation of consular powers and the extradition of criminals, negotiated and ratified here during the last session of Congress, have been accepted and confirmed by the Italian Government. A liberal consular convention which has been negotiated with Belgium will be submitted to the Senate. The very important treaties which were negotiated between the United States and North Germany and Bavaria for the regulation of the rights of naturalized citizens have been duly ratified and exchanged, and similar treaties have been entered into with the Kingdoms of Belgium and Wurtemberg and with the Grand Duchies of Baden and Hesse-Darmstadt. I hope soon to be able to submit equally satisfactory conventions of the same character now in the course of negotiation with the respective Governments of Spain, Italy, and the Ottoman Empire.

Examination of claims against the United States by the Hudsons Bay Company and the Puget Sound Agricultural Company, on account of certain possessory rights in the State of Oregon and Territory of Washington, alleged by those companies in virtue of provisions of the treaty between the United States and Great Britain of June 15, 1846, has been diligently prosecuted, under the direction of the joint international commission to which they were submitted for adjudication by treaty between the two

Governments of July 1, 1863, and will, it is expected, be concluded at an early day.

No practical regulation concerning colonial trade and the fisheries can be accomplished by treaty between the United States and Great Britain until Congress shall have expressed their judgment concerning the principles involved. Three other questions, however, between the United States and Great Britain remain open for adjustment. These are the mutual rights of naturalized citizens, the boundary question involving the title to the island of San Juan, on the Pacific coast, and mutual claims arising since the year 1853 of the citizens and subjects of the two countries for injuries and depredations committed under the authority of their respective Governments. Negotiations upon these subjects are pending, and I am not without hope of being able to lay before the Senate, for its consideration during the present session, protocols calculated to bring to an end these justly exciting and long-existing controversies.

We are not advised of the action of the Chinese Government upon the liberal and auspicious treaty which was recently celebrated with its plenipotentiaries at this capital.

Japan remains a theater of civil war, marked by religious incidents and political severities peculiar to that long-isolated Empire. The Executive has hitherto maintained strict neutrality among the belligerents, and acknowledges with pleasure that it has been frankly and fully sustained in that course by the enlightened concurrence and cooperation of the other treaty powers, namely Great Britain, France, the Netherlands, North Germany, and Italy.

Spain having recently undergone a revolution marked by extraordinary unanimity and preservation of order, the provisional government established at Madrid has been recognized, and the friendly intercourse which has so long happily existed between the two countries remains unchanged.

I renew the recommendation contained in my communication to Congress dated the 18th July last--a copy of which accompanies this message that the judgment of the people should be taken on the propriety of so amending the Federal Constitution that it shall provide--

First. For an election of President and Vice-President by a direct vote of the people, instead of through the agency of electors, and making them ineligible for reelection to a second term.

Second. For a distinct designation of the person who shall discharge the duties of President in the event of a vacancy in that office by the death, resignation, or removal of both the President and Vice-President.

Third. For the election of Senators of the United States directly by the people of the several States, instead of by the legislatures; and

Fourth. For the limitation to a period of years of the terms of Federal judges.

Profoundly impressed with the propriety of making these important modifications in the Constitution, I respectfully submit them for the early and mature consideration of Congress. We should, as far as possible, remove all pretext for violations of the organic law, by remedying such imperfections as time and experience may develop, ever remembering that "the constitution which at any time exists until changed by an explicit and authentic act of the whole people is sacredly obligatory upon all."

In the performance of a duty imposed upon me by the Constitution, I have thus communicated to Congress information of the state of the Union and recommended for their consideration such measures as have seemed to me necessary and expedient. If carried into effect, they will hasten the accomplishment of the great and beneficent purposes for which the Constitution was ordained, and which it comprehensively states were "to form a more perfect Union, establish justice, insure domestic tranquillity, provide for the common defense, promote the general welfare, and secure the blessings of liberty to ourselves and our posterity." In Congress are vested all legislative powers, and upon them devolves the responsibility as well for framing unwise and excessive laws as for neglecting to devise and adopt measures absolutely demanded by the wants of the country. Let us earnestly hope that before the expiration of our respective terms of service, now rapidly drawing to a close, an all-wise Providence will so guide our counsels as to strengthen and preserve the Federal Unions, inspire reverence for the Constitution, restore prosperity and happiness to our whole people, and promote "on earth peace, good will toward men."

CONTENTS

CPSIA information can be obtained
at www.ICGtesting.com
Printed in the USA
LVHW111133140223
739387LV00005B/769